SATI AND THE RIDER

Winslow Eliot

SATI AND THE RIDER

Visit the author website:
winsloweliot.com

Cover design: Tom Stier
tomstier.com

Cover art: Carrie Paris
carrieparis.com

Author website created by promoteglobally.com

Author photo by Sarah Dinan

ISBN: 978-1-939980-08-3 (kindle)
ISBN: 978-1-939980-09-0 (epub)
ISBN: 978-1-939980-06-9 (paperback)
ISBN: 978-1-939980-07-6 (audio)

Published by: Writespa Press
writespa.com

With heartfelt gratitude to

my inspirations,
Sheilaa Hite and Carrie Paris

my zorya,
Nancy Crompton, May Paddock, Samantha Stier

and my friends,
Ginny Guenette, Cristina Hadzi, Claudia Jackson

The Rider:
News, a delivery, a young man, perhaps a lover.
A new person or situation entering your life.
A visit. A horse, a car, or other means of transportation.
Opportunity. Things moving quickly. A vibrant social life.
Elegance. Energy. Comings and goings.
9 of Hearts: A wish fulfilled.
Timing: Soon, in a day, next week, in January.

1. I don't often get men as clients. Usually if a man shows up for a consultation, it's because his girlfriend or wife pushed him to it.

When they do come in, they tend to be reluctant, or skeptical, or nervous.

Sometimes all three.

But Joel Wakefield was different. Not that he was chatty or curious. No, he was chilly and dry as unbuttered toast in an Italian marmalade suit, a beige cashmere coat draped over his arm, fawn leather gloves, somewhere between forty and fifty, with an ultra-smooth chin that jutted aggressively.

He certainly was not reluctant or nervous. He set down his gloves and a manila envelope on the mantel, and frostily asked me to advise him on whether or not he could trust—*completely*—one of his employees.

I like to get to know my clients before I dive right into a reading, so after inviting him to sit down, I asked him what kind of business he was in.

"You're the psychic," he said. "You tell me."

I refrained from making a joke, since he didn't

seem the humorous type, and grew quiet inwardly. I'd been giving readings for people for so long that by now it hardly took more than a minute to grow still inside. When I was ready, I checked a sample of his dubious operative's handwriting, which I had the foresight to ask him to bring. I checked the o's and a's first—no loops. They were closed, too, so I could tell he wasn't much of a talker. But they were clean and clear, so I knew he wasn't hiding anything from his boss.

The answer was unequivocal: yes, his employee, Simon Jones, could be trusted completely.

But I didn't make my answer unequivocal. Whenever I was asked questions of this kind, I really needed to be absolutely sure, because Joel Wakefield implied he was trusting this employee with large sums of money.

And, more importantly, I didn't want him to walk out without paying for the full hour appointment. I seriously needed the money.

So I did a little scrying with the crystal ball, and studied the tarot spread I laid out on the low oak chest between us. The 10 of Swords seemed to vibrate and shift slightly and I turned my attention to it. The exhausted figure sprawled face-down on the hard ground in a pool of crimson. *Something coming to an end.*

I turned back to the handwriting and recognized signs of repressed anger.

Another thing I noticed: the writer was depressed. Aggressive, but I could easily glimpse his feelings of hopelessness and despair. The jagged phrases sloped down to the right—almost off the edge of the page.

But when I began to say some of this out loud, my client reminded me sharply that he was not asking about the mood of his employee. All he was asking was whether or not he could trust him.

"Yes, you can trust him," I said finally, confidently, toward the end of the hour. "Simon Jones is a good guy. Is there anything else you'd like to ask me?"

He assessed me silently, as though I were a department store suit on a hanger. His bronze shoes gleamed in the low light. He was sitting with one leg crossed over his thigh so I could see the shine on the leather sole. It was barely scuffed.

I wondered what he was waiting for, because our hour was up and I was expecting my next client at noon. I glanced at the clock on the wall, making a point. He saw me do it and a dimple creased his cheek as though he was trying to smile but it hurt.

He didn't look like he intended to leave. There was definitely something else on his mind.

"Yes?" I prompted. "There's something else?"

The hostile eyes flickered, almost softened, like a ripple in a pale gray sea. But then they froze again and he said, "Yes, there is. I want you to find my daughter."

2. "What happened to her?" I asked cautiously.

"I hope—" he hesitated, placed the lustrous shoes on the worn carpet and his hard hands on his thighs. "I don't mean that. I don't mean I hope she's run away. But I'd rather that than…" He stopped again.

I knew what he was thinking.

"How old is she?" I asked.

"Nineteen. Almost twenty."

"Has anyone contacted you?"

He gave an almost imperceptible start, as though he'd been caught in a lie.

"You mean for a ransom? No, of course not." Abruptly he reached for the manila envelope and handed it to me. "Her name's Ruby. There's an old photo in there. Some other things, too. Her mother's address—we're divorced. Also, a receipt for a bus ticket, and a necklace she used to wear. It's all I have to go on."

I didn't take the envelope. "Are the police looking for her?"

Impatiently, he dropped the envelope on the oak chest, right on top of the tarot spread.

"Yes, of course. They can't do anything."

"Why not?"

"If she's hiding, they won't be able to find her."

I grew more intrigued. I was sure that Joel Wakefield didn't really need me to find his daughter.

Or maybe he already knew where she was, in which case why was he asking me?

"Who would she be hiding from?" I asked.

"I don't know. No one. But it's possible."

"Not really, unless there's a reason."

He fidgeted, then stood up abruptly. "She didn't get along too well with her mother."

"Okay." I waited. Then, "When did you last see her?"

"Two weeks ago. She's a senior in college. She's brilliant—she's graduating early. That is, if she shows up for her last semester. It starts at the end of January." He swallowed, holding back visible emotion.

My heart contracted for him. There was more to his story, I could tell, and what he wasn't telling me became a wall of pain that separated us.

"I'm so sorry—this must be hard for you. But I don't see how I can help. The police really are experts at this kind of thing." I stood up too. "Today's session is $98."

"That wasn't a session," he scoffed. "I was interviewing you to find out whether or not you're as good as I've heard. You have quite a reputation…" his eyes moved up and down my velour leggings and soft angora top, paused on the amber beads on my chest, then settled in my eyes again. "I was interested to find out more about you. A mutual friend recommended you highly."

I knew who that was—a man I'd dated a few times when I was still living in the Berkshires. He'd emailed me about the recommendation. I felt my cheeks flush.

"I have another client waiting," I said. "You can schedule a new appointment if you'd like to consult with me about something else."

He shoved one finger at a time into his leather gloves. "You knew Jones was on the level the moment you saw his handwriting. Graphology is not magic. You stalled for a whole hour for no reason I can see. But since you say you're psychic, it shouldn't take you more than a few hours to track down my daughter." His eyes were half-closed, glinting. "I thought you were for real."

"I am for real. But I'm not going to claim I can find your daughter unless I really thought I could."

"Why can't you, if you're really psychic?"

I knew he was upset, but his belligerence was intense.

"Mainly because you're not telling me the truth about what happened. Or at least you're not telling me the whole story."

He glared. "Yes, I am."

I shook my head, not bothering to argue.

Abruptly, he asked: "Do you take credit cards?"

"No."

"Then I'll mail you a check. You can start earning it by opening that envelope."

I picked it up and held it out to him. "You need a detective, not a psychic."

Ignoring the envelope, he turned to leave, limping slightly as though his feet hurt in the new shoes. He didn't like me, so I was surprised when he turned and said, "I said I'll send a check. I'll pay for today's session, and I'll pay whatever you want to find Ruby. I'm counting on you. Don't let me down."

The front door slammed behind him. I put the envelope on the mantel and gathered up the cards from the top of the oak chest. I only had five minutes before my next client. I used the time to do some deep, clearing breathing, exhaling Joel Wakefield's domineering and negative energy.

It wasn't just the brand new shoes with the shiny soles that disturbed me.

It was the fact that he said he was counting on me to find his daughter.

3. The new year had begun in snow. Not exciting blizzard-snow, nor pretty, fluffy dry flakes that make your cheeks pink and your eyes sparkle.

No, this snow was wet, heavy, and dark even before it hit the New York City pavement. It fell all day yesterday and it was still falling.

Looking out the bay window, I watched it sink into the drifts by the side of Gay Street. The client who was scheduled to come at noon had canceled her appointment a few minutes before she was due to arrive. I was counting on her check to pay my electric bill. I knew I should charge her for a last-minute cancellation but she was an old friend and I couldn't.

I turned away from the furry gray light outside. The front room that I used as a waiting area for my clients looked drab and bare.

The fact was that the small brownstone was costing more than I could afford. A grateful client had left it to me when she died a few months earlier and I'd moved here from the country. At first it had seemed a dream come true, but owning a house in Greenwich Village turned out to be a millstone if you weren't already something of a millionaire. There were fire marshals and building inspectors and historical society representatives who always seemed to demand that I do something to my house that I couldn't afford. Then the roof started leaking and eventually even the buckets I placed in the top floor bedroom weren't enough to take care of that problem.

Now I slept on a couch on the second floor.

There was a cozy basement apartment below, and when it was rented that would help with some of the bills. But I'd already gone through one brief tenant who'd been a fiasco, and so I was proceeding more cautiously this time.

I decided to close up downstairs for now and save on electricity. Glancing into the office at the back where I did my consultations, I swept my gaze around to make sure I hadn't left any candles lit. It was a sweet room, overlooking a tiny garden tucked in like a pocket between neat brick walls. It even had a real brick fireplace, although that needed repair before I'd be able to use it. The velvet cushions on the second-hand couch—orange, purple, and yellow— were inviting but had an un-sat-on look to them.

Strange that it was so quiet. Back in the Berkshires my consulting business had thrived. At least, up till a year ago.

The oak chest gleamed in the pewter glow, and the manila envelope still lay where Joel Wakefield left it.

I was about to go over to it but just then the doorbell rang. When I peered through the beveled glass on the side of the front door, I saw a UPS delivery man on the stoop outside, punching some numbers into the diad, a package tucked under his arm. His parcel-brown uniform was dark from wet snow.

I unlocked the door. "Hello."

His eyes widened, and it took him a moment to catch his breath.

"Satyana?" The cold air fuzzed around his mouth.

"That's me."

"Nice." He seemed flustered. "Is it the name of a company?"

"No, it's mine," I replied. "I don't have a last name."

He still didn't hand me the package, as though he wanted to go on talking. "What's it mean?"

"It's a Sanskrit word. It has to do with truth—my mom was big into yoga when she had me."

"I love it."

"My friends call me Sati, though."

"Okay, Sati." His eyes were warm and flirty.

Ridiculous, since he had to be half my age, at least. But it felt nice.

A wind picked up, diffused his freezing breath, and pushed past us into the house. I held out my hand for the package. "Do I need to sign?"

"Yep." He finished pressing numbers into the diad and, when I'd signed, he handed me the smallish package, waved cheerfully, and turned.

I knew something was going to happen—and audibly sucked in my breath.

The young man slipped, and tried to grab onto the wrought-iron banister as he tumbled backward down the five stone steps. He almost saved himself at the last minute by twisting around to break his fall, but his foot slid out from under him on the bottom step. He landed on his back, and his head hit the sidewalk.

Then he lay very still.

4. Hastily, I thrust the package between the door and the jamb so I wouldn't get locked out and rushed down the snowy steps to his side.

His eyes were closed. Kneeling in the slush, I put my arm under his head so that it wasn't on the sidewalk.

Please don't be dead.

"Are you okay?" I asked.

"Yep." His eyes fluttered open and then he squeezed them shut again. "Ouch."

I put my arm around his shoulders and helped him sit up slowly. He looked around dizzily and tried to stand. Almost immediately he collapsed on the bottom step, wincing. He put his head on his arms, bowed over.

Alarmed, I watched what seemed like a miniature balloon expanding on the back of his skull.

"Come inside and let me put some ice on that bump."

He glanced up. "Ice? Brrrr."

"Then I'll make you some hot tea. We need to make sure you're okay."

"My truck." He seemed much younger now than he did when he was handing me the package. Sort of helpless and frustrated. He had parked right in front of the house, the wheels touching the curb.

I checked the street hastily and made sure that small cars, at least, could get past on the one-way street without too much difficulty.

His diad was still in the slushy gutter and I picked it up.

"Come on inside," I urged him.

Anxiously, he looked at his watch and I realized he must have a tight schedule. Those package deliverers always did, especially around this time of year. But I was worried about him—that was a nasty fall.

"Just for a few minutes," I insisted. "You need to make sure you're okay to drive."

He stood shakily, and it was only then I realized he'd hurt his ankle more than his head. Leaning against the banister, he selected some keys from a belt loop, pressed a button on one that made the hazards start blinking, and then another so the truck gave a small 'parp' and I knew it was locked.

Grimacing, he hopped on one leg, up each step, holding onto the wrought-iron rail.

I picked up the package from the jamb, and we went inside, the heavy door swinging closed behind us. Propping himself on my shoulder, he let himself be guided in small hops into the office.

"Lie on the couch and put your leg up on this pillow," I said, helping him and turning on the light.

He was wearing heavy hiking boots, which he said he'd rather leave on. "Might be sprained. Won't get the boot back on." His face was drawn with pain.

"Wait here. My kitchen's upstairs. I'll get ice for your head."

Grabbing the package I'd dropped on the bottom stair, I dashed up the stairs and filled the electric kettle with water for tea, then wrapped ice in a thin tea towel for the bump.

He was still resting his head on a velvety pillow, his eyes closed, when I returned. I stood behind him and gently placed the ice on the back of his head.

We stayed like that for several minutes, until I knew the water must have boiled upstairs and the kettle had turned itself off.

Then he shifted and I realized the ice was melting down his neck. I wiped it off and examined the wound, which had shrunk a little.

"What's your name?" I asked.

"Percy." He seemed painfully self-conscious, not flirtatious at all now.

"I'll get us some tea."

Upstairs, I put some chamomile flowers in the teapot, placed it with a cup on a tray, and took it back down.

He wrinkled his nose when he smelled the chamomile.

"What's that?"

"Tea. It's calming. Try it."

While he blew on it, I looked out the window at his truck on the street below and saw no sign of activity. Just the blinking hazard lights, like little orange snowflakes.

"Truck okay?" he asked.

"Yes, it's fine. Don't worry."

"I am worried. I really have to get going."

"Drink your tea first."

I went back upstairs, wishing I had cookies or toast or something to offer him to eat. I took out my last precious bar of orange peel chocolate from the refrigerator.

Back downstairs I offered him a piece.

He enjoyed the chocolate more than the tea, and grew less ruffled at finding himself in this predicament.

"Your house?" he asked curiously, his mouth full of chocolate.

"Yes. A client left it to me when she died. She was grateful to me for something I did for her, years ago… I just moved in recently."

"Wow. Lucky. What kind of client was she? I mean, what did you do for her?"

"I tell fortunes," I smiled at him.

5. "Huh?" Percy looked more stunned than when he'd fallen backward onto the sidewalk.

"Yes, her ex-husband accused of doing something she didn't do. She was going to lose everything, including this house. I was able to help her figure out what really happened."

"How?"

"Oh, I use this and that. Cards. A crystal ball. Some people just want me to read their palms."

"And it works?"

I hesitated. "Oh, it works all right."

He held out his hand to me, palm up. It used to be that people did that and something inside would pour through me: I'd know just what needed to be said. But it had been a whole year since that had happened.

I didn't want to tell him that though. *Maybe this time…*

Well, I'd do my best, which nowadays felt like guess-work. I drew up my chair and examined his hand. His fingers seemed delicate for a delivery-man, the pads sensitive. I was struck by his heart line most of all, and then half-closed my eyes to feel its warmth. "You are a messenger—but it's not packages I see you bringing...something else. Do you work with technology—I see connections of a sharp, new different sort for you. And definitely a move—are you thinking of moving? Leaving the city, maybe? There's definitely a move, and perhaps a love affair— is that what is drawing you somewhere else? You *are* in love, aren't you?"

His face was red, but he laughed good-naturedly and withdrew his hand. "Wrong on every count," he said firmly.

"Oh, well. Can't win them all."

"How'd you get into fortune-telling?" he asked.

"I've always done it, or at least something like it. It's a passion."

"And a business?"

"Yes, I've supported myself as a consultant since I was in my mid-twenties. A few years ago, when I discovered a local politician's secreted imbursements, I became something of a celebrity and things started going really well."

"'Secreted imbursements?'"

"That's what *he* called them—I figured it was a discreet way of saying 'girlfriends'. Turned out I was right."

His eyes twinkled. "Are you really psychic? Do you hear voices?"

I hesitated. "I used to," I said. "Not a real voice— more like a message. Or like a fluid light in me. Anyway, there are all sorts of ways of being intuitive. Everyone is, in some way."

"I'm not."

"Well, it takes practice to hone it, and trust it. You might get a gut feeling, for example."

"Do you actually look into a crystal ball?"

"Sometimes. It's a tool that can help. Tarot cards are great too, and palms, although that didn't work too well with you. Lenormand cards…"

"What are they?"

"Fortune-telling cards from the 19th century. They're symbols—a house, a fox, a ring—that sort of thing. There are thirty-six of them."

"Interesting." Percy put the last piece of orange peel chocolate in his mouth. "Okay, I'm off." He rose, gingerly testing his weight on his ankle. Then he collapsed back on the couch.

"What is it?" I rushed over.

"Feels worse."

"Oh no." It was impossible for me to tell, since he still had his boot on, but I got the feeling that it hurt more than he was showing. "I'm going to call an ambulance. You need it x-rayed."

"But my truck. Deliveries."

"You can't drive with that ankle."

He seemed really upset. "Guess I'll have to find a sub."

I lifted his leg back up on the couch while he got on his phone. I called for an ambulance on mine, and covered him with a fleece throw. After a very short conversation, he slipped his phone back in his shirt pocket.

"Is there anyone else you want to call?" I asked. "A friend to meet you at the hospital?"

He shook his head.

"Where do you live?"

"Coney Island. Five floor walk-up." He looked paler and younger.

"What about your parents? Where do they live?"

"Florida."

I sat with him until the ambulance arrived. His eyes were closed and we didn't talk. Then, while the EMT crew prepared the gurney for him, he asked whether I'd hold on to the keys to the truck and the diad. Someone from UPS would be there shortly.

"Sorry—big favor," he said. "I'll repay you."

"It's nothing, I'm glad to." Even though it wasn't my fault, I felt responsible. They *were* my steps he fell down. "Percy, what's your phone number? I'll check on you later."

He rattled it off and I quickly entered it into my phone. He settled on the gurney, the EMT crew strapped him down, and he was gone. Not much later another UPS delivery man—much grumpier than Percy was—rang my doorbell, took the keys and diad, and set off with the truck.

The house seemed extra quiet and empty after so much commotion. I closed the door to the office, and went upstairs. I would have liked a glass of sparkling wine, but there was none left. I knew I could call Avery or Brigitte—either one of them would gladly bring me a bottle to share. But I couldn't. It was so different calling a friend to bring some cheer when you knew you could reciprocate.

I gave myself a shake and drew the curtains against the late afternoon gloom.

My eyes swiveled to the package Percy had delivered that I'd dropped on the table earlier. I hadn't had a chance to look at the return address yet, so I went over and picked it up.

It was from Leandros. My heart gave a little skip when I saw his name. He sent me things occasionally, sometimes expensive, sometimes a joke, sometimes meaningful. Our relationship had been like that for a long time. We'd grown up together, we fell in love, and he screwed up. That was all there was to it—he knew it, I knew it, and we never talked about it.

The package was too light to be what I really wanted: a bottle of sparkling wine from somewhere off the Costa Brava where he'd been vacationing with his family.

Instead, inside I discovered a smallish rectangular box wrapped in red and gold. It was about the size of a large chocolate bar and I grew hopeful. I could use some, since Percy had eaten all I had.

I untied the gold ribbon, opened the red paper, and discovered a thick envelope.

No chocolate. My heart subsided. Probably one of his jokey cards.

I opened the envelope.

Inside were seven one hundred dollar bills.

My breath caught. *No way.* Why would he send me money? Had I hinted that things were tight for me?

I couldn't have—I *never* would do that.

I fanned the bills and waved them gently in front of my cheek.

Crisp.

New: the image of modest Ben Franklin took up almost the entire bill, from top to bottom.

Greenish.

Exuding that unique aroma of meadow, pocket, stale living room, and old castle that only money has.

Well, for whatever reason, he sent me money. And at least it looked like I'd be able to get that wine after all.

6. I texted my best friends, Brigitte and Avery. Brigitte was eager to join me and offered to pick up Prosecco and Thai take-out. Avery was singing at a club somewhere in Brooklyn, but said she would drop by on her way home if we were still partying.

I'd known Brigitte since college. She used to be a set designer for the Metropolitan Opera; her current occupation was interior designer. She knew all kinds of famous people, and she was one of the most stylish people I'd ever met.

Tonight she wore grey suede, lace-trimmed gloves, a matching hat with grey roses, and a tiny scrap of stretchy material around her thighs. Her thigh-high boots were black and grey alligator, with shiny studs on the toe and heel. They were breathtaking, I admitted when she asked, and I meant it. She was the only person I knew who could walk out in snow like she was in a fashion shoot for Vogue, instead of bedraggled and mucousy.

She had brought me a new pair of gloves. One of her clients was a glove-maker, which was turning out very well for me. Tonight's were black velvet, with tiny silver embroidered teardrops trailing down the thumb to the mound of Venus and lacing the wrist.

"They're gorgeous," I said, shoving my sweater sleeves up and tugging the velvet to my elbows. They fitted, literally, 'like a glove.' Because all the gloves she gave me were so gorgeous, and I had so many of them, I'd gotten into the habit of always wearing a pair, except when I was inside my house. Some people thought that was peculiar, but by now I felt strange without them, even in summer.

Two hours later we were both feeling much more cheerful. Brigitte didn't have any challenges money-wise, but she was constantly entangled in messy relationships. I told her what happened with the UPS deliverer and she was immediately intrigued.

"Potential?" she asked in her faint Texan drawl.

"He's cute," I admitted. "But too young."

"I don't mind," she winked.

"Pshaw." I poured us more bubbles, which neither of us needed. But they sure felt tasty on the palate.

When she asked how my business was going I said, "Pretty good," and she knew what that meant.

"If you could just let people know how great you are…" she exclaimed. She was one of my most ardent enthusiasts.

"And if I could invoice the ones who do come. I keep giving away consultations for free."

"You *shouldn't.*"

"I know. Guess what happened this afternoon?" I described the client with the swanky shoes who had initially refused to pay me.

She was encouragingly outraged. But she also believed I could do more to build up my consulting business.

"You *have* to let me decorate your office," she said. "I have so many old things in storage. You need to make it look sharp—professional. Give the appearance of being a pro."

"I know, and I couldn't have anyone better than you to help me."

But I knew I had to be careful about letting Brigitte take over the interior decorating of my house. It wasn't that I didn't love her sense of style and I knew I could trust her to dress my house exquisitely. It was that people had a tendency to want to do things for me that went way beyond the edges of regular old generosity. Sometimes I felt I had to refuse their help or offerings simply to protect them from themselves.

"Then let's do it!" she urged. "I have stuff in storage that's been there for years."

Knowing Brigitte, it was probably valuable. "Maybe you could sell some of it."

"Ha! You of all people know when it's time to just pass something along. I *know* those old pieces belong here."

"Well, we'll see. It's a wonderful offer."

I called Percy's cell phone at eight o'clock, figuring that a diagnosis must have been made by then. He was very glum. "Fractured, needs a cast. Can't put one on 'cos there's too much swelling. They don't want me to stay 'cos of insurance. Trying to find out if UPS'll cover it. But can't go home because of all those stairs. Sucks."

I met Brigitte's eyes and covered the phone. "He's got nowhere to go. They can't put the cast on yet because it's so swollen."

Her darkly made-up eyes gleamed. "Have him come here," she commanded. "I want to meet him."

I hesitated, because he was a stranger after all. But I also felt sure about him—that he was an okay person. I heard myself say into the phone: "Percy, get a cab and come here, okay? You can sleep on the couch in my office. That way you only have to make your way up the stoop. They'll give you crutches, right?"

Silence. Then, "What?"

"Why not?"

"You don't know me—I'll call a friend." He sounded weak and faint and that made me even more determined to take care of him.

"You fell off my stoop. I feel responsible."

"Not your fault."

"Percy, don't argue. The address is 22 Gay Street. Can you get a cab?" When he didn't say anything I added, "I have a friend here—we can help you up the front steps."

I realized Brigitte was nodding approvingly at me, her pretty mouth in a bow-shaped smile.

Percy's painkillers must have kicked in, because he took me up on my offer without any more polite resistance.

"Okay. Thanks."

7. When he arrived an hour or so later he seemed as pale and wan as any knight in a romantic ballad. I could tell that even Brigitte, who didn't read Keats as I do, felt the same way.

We helped him onto the couch and he manfully tried to pretend he was not in a great deal of pain. Pampering him was great fun for both of us. We brought him soup, toast, and tea and Brigitte urged him to take another Percocet so he could rest more comfortably.

Eventually, he seemed ready to doze, so we turned off the light, closed the door, and left him alone. I told him if he needed anything in the night, he could call my cell.

It was almost midnight by this point and Brigitte took off reluctantly. She was a night owl and loved this kind of activity. But I needed my sleep so I said goodbye to her on the stoop, reminding her to be extra careful as she walked down the steps in her four-inch heels.

With a wave, she headed toward Waverly Place.

Gay Street was almost always quiet in the middle of the night, except sometimes in the height of summer. It wasn't snowing anymore and my breath fogged the night air. I could hear the traffic from Sixth Avenue and beyond.

Sliding shut the night bolt, I hesitated then went to the closed office door. I couldn't hear anything, so I assumed Percy had already fallen asleep, but what if he hadn't? What if he was lying in there, suffering and lonely?

My tender side made me softly turn the handle of the door and peek inside.

He was propped up on the pillows and his eyes were wide open, facing me. He made no sign that he saw me and I figured the Percocet numbed him a little.

"Just checking," I smiled, turning on the overhead light. "You okay?"

"Yep. Thanks so much for letting me stay over." He was flushing again. "I'll take a cab home tomorrow."

"I thought you said you live five flights up."

He sighed grimly. "Yep, it sure is a relief to be here tonight."

It was Thursday night and I didn't have any clients scheduled till Monday. By then his swelling would have subsided, he'd get his cast on, and he could find his way home much more easily.

Impulsively, I decided: "Why don't you plan on staying the weekend? Once you get your cast you'll be able to get around on your crutches. If you try to climb up five flights of stairs, it'll be weeks before the swelling goes down enough for you to get that cast."

He was grateful, but obviously felt it was a huge imposition. "See how I feel tomorrow," was all he would agree to.

I still didn't feel like leaving him alone. I glanced around the room, as though I was looking for something, and my eyes fell on the manila envelope that Joel Wakefield left earlier. I went over to it, as if that was what I came in for.

"Ah—here it is."

"What?"

"A client left this with me earlier. His daughter is missing and he wants me to try to find her." I wasn't sure why I was telling him.

But his eyes flickered with cynical interest.

"You can find missing people?" he asked.

"Probably not," I admitted. "I told the client I couldn't. But he insisted and left me this anyway. And I do need the money, and he said he'd pay whatever I asked."

Percy looked even more interested. "What would you charge?"

"I have no idea. I've never done anything like this before." I sat on the arm of the lumpy armchair, the manila envelope in my hand, my legs swinging in the fluffy slippers. There was a great, sleepy, cozy, middle-of-the-night warm feeling in the room. "Anyway, he still owes me for today's session. He didn't pay me yet."

"How much do you charge for regular old consults?"

I told him, but then added, "I don't always charge

though. Sometimes people just don't have the money but I know they need my help."

Curiously, he glanced around. I could see it was hard for him to figure out how well off I was, with the few pieces of furniture, walls that needed painting, but I lived in such a great location. "Can you afford to do that?"

"Not really." I smiled at him again. There was something so sweet about him. "I moved here recently. I'm still getting used to it all."

"Where'd you move from?"

"The Berkshires. A couple of hours north."

"And you told fortunes there too?"

"Yes, and I was doing really well, too. Then—things happened. And I ended up moving."

"Maybe you need to rent out a part of it."

"There's a small apartment in the basement. The tenant skipped out last week, but as soon as I have someone new in there things will get better."

He looked exasperated. "Have a security deposit?"

"I spent that on repairing the bathroom plumbing—something was wrong with it. And I've been down with flu for a couple of weeks so I'm behind on a lot of things." I looked down at the manila envelope in my hand, then set it back on the oak chest. "I'd have to believe I'd be successful, though, before I agreed to try to find her."

"Can you be?"

"I don't know for sure." I wasn't sure whether I wanted to tell him the truth: that I hadn't felt sure about my intuitive power for a year.

He closed his eyes.

"Maybe it just takes logic."

8. "What about you?" I changed the subject. "Why UPS?"

"I want to start my own business eventually. But I have to pay back student loans first."

He yawned, so I did too, realizing how tired I was. I stood up, left Joel Wakefield's envelope on the chest, and stretched.

"Have everything you need for now? I'll see you in the morning."

"Good night, and thanks again." He seemed already half-asleep.

I slept fitfully, in spite of being so tired, and that meant when I finally awoke cloudy daylight streamed through the front window that overlooked Gay Street. It was already eight o'clock. I immediately got up and grabbed my robe, my mind on my guest downstairs. Was he awake? Was he okay?

I checked my phone and saw he hadn't texted or called. Maybe he was still asleep.

In the kitchen area I filled the electric kettle to make coffee.

The house was small: My kitchen and living

room were all one room on the second floor, and
there was a tiny bathroom with a shower. The
bedroom with the leaky ceiling was above me. It was
half the size of my second floor because it opened
onto a roof terrace. Next summer I planned to grow
tomatoes and morning glories out there.

Then there was the office on the first floor, with a
largish entryway, and a toilet and sink under the
stairs. The basement—or garden, as I preferred to call
it—apartment was even smaller, because the
plumbing and heater took up space at the back of the
house. I didn't go in there much—when there was a
problem I hired a handyman, Quentin, who took care
of it.

While the coffee was brewing and the toast was
toasting, I got dressed. Then I took the tray
downstairs. Percy was awake, the contents of the
manila envelope spread on the blanket on his lap.

"Hello," I said. "I brought you coffee."

"Thanks." He piled everything together and
placed it back in the envelope. "You left this here,
and it wasn't sealed, so I thought I'd take a look."

"Any ideas?"

"Some." He seemed grateful for the coffee and
toast. As he munched, he eyed me questioningly. "I
think I could help you find her."

I looked at him, surprised and curious. "Really?"

"She's probably a runaway. If it wasn't for my
ankle, I could track her down within a day."

"How can you be sure?"

"Kind of straightforward. Item one: divorced
parents. Item two: she's a senior in college, and she's

graduating in May. Item three: mother kicked her out four years ago because she caught her smoking pot at home. That's when she moved in with dad. Item four: they fight—probably something to do with her college. Maybe he threatened not to pay for it. Item five: she disappears soon afterward, but she's bought her own bus ticket. She wasn't kidnapped."

I looked at him with admiration. "You got all that from one envelope?"

"Yep."

"Well, you're right about her parents being divorced. Joel Wakefield told me."

I jumped off the armchair and went over to examine the contents. When I'd laid them out on top of the oak chest, I tried to make the same sense of them that Percy had. All I saw was a receipt for a Greyhound bus ticket, a phone bill, a receipt for a youth hostel, two receipts for McDonald's, a bank account, and a silver chain with an Egyptian ankh pendant. There was also a semi-blurry photo of a girl much younger than nineteen. She had a square face, with wide naive eyes, reddish hair.

I looked up. "I don't know how you pieced together your theory from this."

"Took some doing," he said modestly.

I waited for him to elucidate, but he didn't, just sipped his coffee.

"Come on," I prodded. "Tell me."

"Why would he give you her mother's address if they weren't divorced? Her address on her college i.d. is her father's, so I assume she lived with him. Well, why wouldn't she live with her mother? She was probably kicked out … I'm guessing that part, and the pot-smoking. Her bank statement shows a nice allowance, but the youth hostel means she doesn't have much money—did her father cut off that allowance? And is he paying her entire ride at the college? We could start by contacting the administrator there."

"I'm sure the police have already done that." But I was impressed. "What about the pendant?"

He surprised me by saying, "I thought maybe you could get a feeling from that. What do you think?"

I picked up the chain, and gazed at the ankh. Then I let it rest in the center of my palm, my eyes closed. I had spent a couple of years in India, studying with a guru who taught me how to 'see' using the palm of my hand, and I liked to practice whenever I could.

Quiet filled me and I felt empty but not in a good way. "Sad," I murmured. "Lost. And she feels imprisoned, but not in the normal sense. I wonder …"

"Go on."

"I think she's looking for this. Wondering where it is." I opened my eyes and turned the pendant over. "It says 'wheat' on the back. What does that mean?"

He shrugged. "Dunno."

I was intrigued. "Maybe we could find her. How much would we charge?"

"A lot. He obviously really cares about finding her."

I glanced at the pendant again. "How do you

know?"

"The fact he wants to hire you. He's the kind of person who would only ask a psychic if he was frantic."

Joel Wakefield might be a jerk, but Percy was right: he was desperate to find his daughter. There was a heart in that darkness, somewhere.

"Okay, I'll try to find his daughter and you'll help."

"How about if we bill him for $5,000 plus expenses."

I laughed.

"I'm serious. Do you take credit cards?"

I shook my head, still smiling.

"He can pay through PayPal. Have an account?"

I knew about PayPal, but I'd never set up an account. Technical stuff was not my forte.

"I'll set you up," Percy said. "We'll invoice him this morning for that consultation he still owes you for. Once he's paid for that, you'll say you'll find his daughter for $5,000 plus expenses. He can pay half up front and half when you find her. You have his email, right? A computer? A laptop?"

I nodded, swept up in his energy and directness. I was sure Joel Wakefield would balk at the price, but I had nothing to lose by asking.

"Okay, I'll bring it down and you can fix me up with an account." I smiled at him. "What about you? Need anything?"

He looked awkward. "One of my roommates said he'd bring over a few things later. A toothbrush and my laptop is what I miss most. Texted him earlier.

Hope that's okay."

"Of course. I said you can stay till Monday. That's when they'll put the cast on, right?"

"Hope so."

I brought my computer down, put it on his lap, and he rapidly and expertly tapped the keys. Within a few minutes I had a PayPal account, and he had invoiced Joel Wakefield.

I was really starting to like this guy.

9. Snow had begun falling while we were talking, and when I checked the weather I learned we might get a foot of snow overnight. Better get more Prosecco and something for dinner before the shelves were cleaned out. I'd been meaning to try a sesame noodle recipe that Avery had given me. It had been on my fridge for months.

It wasn't yet ten o'clock, but Percy looked ready to doze again, so I put on my cloak and ventured outside. Everyone else was buying eggs, bread, milk, and toilet paper. I was sure the cashier thought I was a weirdo as she swiped my sesame noodles, kale, and tempeh. At the last minute I grabbed toilet paper and chocolate chip cookies too.

The snow was falling fast by now, and I was exhilarated as I headed home. My stoop was already plastered with it, and I set the groceries inside the front door and swept it clean, grateful that Quentin had already shoveled the sidewalk. My neighbors hired him to shovel theirs, and he said it wasn't any bother to do mine at the same time.

I went inside, hung my snow-soaked cloak on the hook, and poked my head into the office where Percy was.

"He paid the $98," he announced, grinning broadly at me.

"You're kidding!"

"Nope. Here it is. He paid as soon as he got the invoice, about an hour ago. Now we can bill him the $5,000 to find his daughter."

I didn't think he was serious, but there was no harm in trying, so I told him to go ahead.

While I'd been out, Percy's friend had brought his computer and some clothes, and Percy had changed into a dark red sweater and black sweatpants. He seemed fresher.

"Hungry?" I asked.

"Yep."

"I'll start an early lunch."

"I can get up the stairs," he insisted, reaching for his crutches.

"That'll make your ankle swell up, and then you won't get your cast on Monday," I said sternly. "Stay where you are."

He reluctantly subsided on the couch.

"I'm making us sesame noodles. They don't take long. I'll be right back."

"Awesome. Thanks."

I left him the box of cookies and went upstairs.

When I brought him the dish, he closed the top of his notebook, set it next to mine on the oak chest, and sat up to eat. He seemed to like the sesame noodles a lot. I'd barely had a few bites of mine by the time he'd finished.

I refilled his plate, while he drank down a glass of almond milk. When he was finished he looked ready to doze again and I left him to go upstairs and try a new knitting pattern for a sweater.

At three-thirty, I was making a pot of tea for myself when he texted me.

"Joel Wakefield says okay."

I let out a screech and raced downstairs.

"Yep," Percy read out loud when I entered the office. "'Transferring money now'."

My jaw was on my chest and I used a forefinger to prop it back to its normal position. "*Did* he transfer it?"

Percy frowned. "Yep. What's weird, though, is that he gave you the whole $5,000. I assumed he'd send half up front, as a retainer, and half when we found his daughter. I think he really wants your help—and fast. We'd better get to work."

I stared. Then I said cautiously, "I agree that I need to find her. There's something about why Joel Wakefield asked me…but I'm not sure how to go about it."

"How about if you do the intuitive part and I'll put the logical pieces together. We've figured out a lot already."

"Yes, that she's a runaway?" I wasn't even sure if

that was true.

We were looking at each other and I thought he was going to give me some encouragement about how intuitive he truly believed I was, but instead he said:

"Look, I can't work for UPS for six weeks at least. I'm stuck and broke. Disability won't cover much." He leaned close. "Hire me. I'll help you find Ruby Wakefield."

10. Back in the Middle Ages when rye or barley or other grain was typically used as a floor covering, people would place a low board to keep the dried grass from spilling into other rooms or outside. At a threshold moment, the board was removed, and the grain flowed from the confines of a single room.

At least that's one theory about the origin of "threshold moment."

I've thought about threshold moments a lot. We have so many of them in our lifetimes.

I'd met this young man less than twenty-four hours ago. He'd been delivering a package, and he fell off my stoop. Now he was confined to my room, because I invited him in a fit of remorse. As though I made him slip, not his own clumsiness.

Relationships happen this way, more often than

we realize. Someone gives you their seat on the subway. A child drops his toy on the sidewalk and you pick it up and you've created a relationship.

As I continued to gaze at Percy, thinking these things, I imagined a golden glow surrounding him. After a moment, I realized he'd moved the floor lamp earlier so that it was behind him.

He looked back, not eagerly, not pleadingly, but with a sort of calm expectation that *this is the way it was meant to be.*

I had nothing to lose by agreeing.

So I agreed.

Then I spoke without thinking.

"Maybe you can get me more clients too, while you're at it. Get my accounts in order. Sort of be my business manager. Didn't you say you wanted to have your own business one day? This could be practice."

He looked unsure. "What do you mean?"

"What I said. Get me clients. Work out a budget. Figure out my bills and how I'm going to pay them."

I could tell he was interested. "How much did you say you charge? $98 a session?" He scrunched his forehead. "How many clients could you see in a day?"

Since for the past year I hadn't been able to scrounge up more than one even on a really good day, I wasn't sure how to answer.

"If they're hour-long sessions, maybe two in the morning, not too early. And two or three in the afternoon?"

"Wouldn't five clients in a day wear you out?"

"It might. But not having any money wears me out more."

"If you had five clients a day, that's five hundred—twenty-five hundred a week—you could be making ten thousand a month, easily."

"You think you could get me five clients a day?"

"Well, maybe not five. Start with two."

"How much?"

"How much what?"

"How much would you want?"

He saw I was serious, and propped himself up on the cushions. "Commission. Adds incentive. We could do some local advertising. We'll also set you up on some social media sites. I noticed you don't have accounts, and they're good marketing tools."

Our eyes met again and something in his pierced me. I hadn't seen that look in years. Not since Leandros... *stop it.*

I gently removed the sense that his hands were closing around my heart.

He's just a boy, I reminded myself.

"Well, go for it. Good luck. We'll see what happens. What's your commission?"

"Twenty-five percent," he said, this time without hesitating. "Covers not only getting clients, but taking care of your business, including the books. If I get you $10,000 a month, I'd get to keep twenty-five hundred. Fair?"

I tried to hold onto even a shred of skepticism. What if this was some horrible elaborate scam? I *couldn't* let a stranger have complete access to all my financial information.

He nodded again, quickly, as though he could read my mind. "I have references. Worked for UPS past three years. Talk to my landlord: always paid rent. Talk to my roommates. Give you my parents' number in Florida. Mom likes me so she's prejudiced but might make you feel better. Graduated from college three years ago."

"Where did you go?" I asked.

"Boston."

Well, I wasn't all that savvy with technical gadgets, but I knew I could discover whether he paid his rent on time, whether his parents lived in Florida, and whether or not he graduated from college three years ago. I could also find out about his employment record at UPS. Those were all bits and pieces of a person's life that made him substantial and trustworthy. People didn't change all that much. If he'd planned on embezzling the UPS, he would have done it by now. If he cheated on exams, he would've been found out by now.

"Okay."

"Just like that? Aren't you going to read your cards or something?"

"Do you want me to?"

"No, I don't buy that crap."

"How are you going to get me clients if you don't believe in me?"

His eyes were darling. "I believe in *you*, not the cards."

The doorbell rang and I went to see who it might be on this snowy late Friday afternoon. I peered through the glass and saw a man in a paste-colored raincoat and fedora with a cop standing beside him.

Uh-oh.

Even when one was entirely innocent, it was a shock to have to open the door to a police officer. My first thought was that Percy was a con man and they had traced him to my home in the nick of time.

"May I help you?"

"Satyana? No last name?"

"That's me."

"I'm Detective Cleveland, ma'am. This is Officer Blesson. May we come in?"

11. Even knowing I hadn't done anything wrong, I felt nervous. Detective Cleveland was dark, unshaven, grizzled, with heavy, protruding eyebrows, and an angry expression. The police officer was sternly impassive.

They stamped their snowy boots hard on the mat inside my door, and I showed them into my office. Percy nodded politely at the two men and didn't look at all nervous, so I figured it wasn't him they were after.

"Percy, my business associate," I introduced him. "What's this about?"

"Do you know a Mr. Joel Wakefield?"

Uh-oh.

"I met him once. He came for a consultation yesterday."

The detective's dark eyes were darting everywhere, like I imagined those secret service eyes did behind the sunglasses when they were protecting a VIP. "What kind of consultation?"

"I do intuitive readings for people."

The uniformed officer remained poker-faced but the detective did not pretend to hide a sneer. He glared at me from under the gray eyebrows that were like concrete window ledges.

"Mr. Wakefield gave you a great deal of money for a reading."

"I charge ninety-eight dollars per session," I said stiffly. "I don't call that a great deal of money, I call it fair."

Percy nodded warmly in assent.

"We have evidence that Mr. Wakefield transferred $5,000 into your PayPal account earlier today. Can you tell us what that was for?"

I gawped.

"Mr. Wakefield hired me to find his missing daughter," I said, a little less confidently. "I charge more in those cases."

The cynicism on the detective's face was insulting. I turned to Percy for help, but he was looking at me with eyes so warm I flushed.

"The police have been searching for Joel Wakefield's daughter for two weeks without success," Mr. Detective stated abruptly. "You think you'd be luckier? Have any leads?"

I didn't have to answer him, I knew that. But I

was curious about why he was here. Joel Wakefield surely gave the police the same information he gave me, so it couldn't be that he just wanted the manila envelope lying beside Percy.

"No," I said slowly.

"Then what was that $5,000 he gave you for?"

"He just paid that a couple of hours ago. I haven't started working yet."

The detective glanced at the police officer, then at Percy, then back at me. His eyes were tough as truck tires.

"He couldn't have paid you. Mr. Joel Wakefield was murdered earlier this morning, several hours before the transfer was made."

12. My eyes met Percy's, startled, across the room.

"Murdered!" we said in unison.

"What happened to him?" I asked.

Detective Cleveland looked at each of us in turn, glowering, his heavy eyebrows lifting and then sinking. "He was shot in a coffee shop while he was eating. Happened at 10 a.m. There are at least fifteen witnesses. He died on his way to the hospital."

Awful. My immediate thought was for his daughter Ruby ... did she know? Had she heard?

"So he couldn't have transferred the money," I said, half to myself. "Who did?"

He swung back to me. "That's what we'd like to find out."

"Have you caught the person who killed him?"

"Not yet. Do *you* know who it is?"

I really did not like this man. I knew I could summon my magic Voice and completely disarm him, but instead I didn't answer.

"What was that $5,000 for?" he insisted, taking a step toward me.

"To find Joel Wakefield's daughter, Ruby."

"How do you propose do that?"

"He gave me some clues to get me started." I gestured to Percy and he handed the manila envelope to me to give to Mr. Detective, who handed it to Mr. Police Officer without looking at it.

I was sorry to watch its contents depart, but there was no point in keeping it now.

I doubted I'd be able to keep the $5,000 either.

"What else did Mr. Wakefield ask you?" Mr. Detective demanded. "What was the consultation about? Surely you didn't merely chat about his daughter?"

I didn't want to betray client confidentiality, even if the client was dead, so I decided not to mention Joel Wakefield's initial question about his employee's moral fiber.

"Mr. Wakefield wanted to get to know me before he hired me," I said slowly. "He wanted to find out if he could trust me. He seemed desperate to find his daughter. Maybe he saw me as a last resort, or maybe he thought I could help him more than the police could."

Mr. Detective harrumphed, scowled, and paced edgily around the room, rubbing his unshaved chin. He irked me, but maybe it was because I didn't like his innuendo that I was somehow involved with a murderer.

He stopped in front of me and thrust his face close to mine. "We don't know who transferred the money, but whoever it was must have some sort of tie to you. We have to get to the bottom of this."

I didn't budge. "I hope you do."

"Maybe you know something? Maybe you're in cahoots?" His eyebrows were just inches from mine. "Is there anything else you want to tell us now? I'm warning you, next time we talk it might be in the Tombs."

I knew he was referring to jail, not a mausoleum, but I shivered nonetheless. I was out of my depth. I longed to do a spread and get some insight into the situation, but it was not the right time—not as long as Mr. Tough-Eyes was there.

"I'll be glad to cooperate in any way I can," I assured him, calmly. "But I really don't see how I can help. I never met the man before yesterday. I don't even know where he lives."

I was hugely relieved when Detective Cleveland said they were going to leave. I walked them to the front door, and hastily grabbed the broom to sweep the stoop clear of snow before they slipped. But the stony-faced police officer thawed and took it from me to do the job himself. The detective waited inside the snowy squad car, the manila envelope on his lap.

When the officer handed me back the broom, I smiled warmly. "Thank you so much."

He actually smiled back. "You take care now, okay?"

Then he got in the driver's side and they drove off.

I closed the door, drew the bolt.

"You okay?" Percy asked when I went back inside the office. "You look shaky."

"That was kind of spooky," I admitted.

"I know." He was puzzled. "Strange you'd be paid—entire amount—*after* Wakefield's murdered. If I were a homicide detective, I'd wonder."

"I'd wonder even if I wasn't a homicide detective. What do we do now? Should we offer to give the money back?"

"Already moved to your bank account," he said. "Better wait on that."

Our eyes met again, and I knew what he was thinking. *Ruby*.

"Yes, I might need it to try to find her. But now they've taken the envelope with all those clues, I don't even know where to begin. Where was the bus ticket for?"

"San Francisco."

"Oh, that's right."

Percy gave me a weird look, like he wasn't telling me something.

"What?" I said.

"You didn't put the pendant back. Still here." He reached behind him under a yellow pillow, and pulled out the silver ankh. "Here you go."

I took it, not sure what to do with it. "Not much to go on."

"Hope you don't mind," he looked modestly down. "I snapped a few pictures of everything else that was inside the envelope. I know you didn't tell me to, but I wanted to study them and thought you might give it back to your client. That was before I knew he was dead."

13. I stared. He wasn't sure if I was mad or impressed.

I wasn't sure either.

He leaned back against the cushions, eyes closed. He looked pretty beat. I couldn't believe how much had happened in less than twenty-four hours. Absently, I reached for my lenormand cards and laid a *petit tableau* on my lap, wondering what it all meant: a murdered client, Percy's accident, sudden money sent from my best friend…

Reading the lenormand cards is different from reading the tarot. They are much more precise—I use them more as a tracking device or an actual map than for personal exploration. For instance, when I needed to tie something together in story form, as I did now.

The first card was the Snake, which made me

nervous, but that was quickly followed by Lilies. Okay, letting go. Some sort of solution. "Lilies" was most likely my old friend Leandros. Or could it be Joel Wakefield, even though he was dead?

Beside the Lilies was the Anchor. A legacy, or inheritance.

The second row consisted of the Stork, the Rider, and the Heart. On the bottom I turned over the Broom, the House, and some happy-looking Fish.

As my eyes were drawn to the various combinations in the three-by-three spread, I felt my shoulders relax. My gaze flowed diagonally from the Lilies to the Rider and the Fish. I was moving out of stagnation, through dint of a new force of energy in my life (Rider) and financial success (Fish) seemed assured. The Stork beside the Rider augured a major change, and the Heart suggested new friendships. The Broom exhorted me to sternly apply myself to a new course.

The House directly under the Rider made me glance up at the young man lying on the couch across from me with his eyes closed.

His breathing grew even, and I looked back at the cards, letting them weave themselves together in imagery and significance. I didn't always have to come to a conclusion—sometimes looking at the lenormand cards was like reading a poem or a stream-of-consciousness short story. After a while I put them away and reached over for his phone which Percy had placed beside his empty plate. Swiping through the photos, I saw images for the receipt for the Greyhound bus ticket to San Francisco, the pendant with the ankh. The photograph of a girl with a squarish face, smiling bravely, reddish-blond hair. She was small and slight.

There were a few other images: her college i.d., a photo of the entrance to a youth hostel. There was a photo of something I couldn't make out. Looked like a crushed candy wrapper.

The girl's bank account statement was interesting. There were regular weekly withdrawals of $50, going back about a year.

I flipped through all the photos again as though I was fanning cards in front of me. They zipped by me like one of those flipbooks. But nothing was getting any clearer. Just the realization that this poor girl's father was dead.

My heart ached for her. Did she know? Had she heard?

There had to be a connection here: he was looking for his missing daughter and then he died.

But what was the connection?

14.

Percy gave a snort in his sleep and I covered him with a fleece throw. My phone buzzed again and I saw that Leandros was trying to get hold of me. Was he back from his vacation?

I tiptoed out of the office, went upstairs, then

called him back.

"Are you home?" I asked.

"Yes, got back a few days ago."

"Have fun?"

"Lots." I could hear the smile in his voice so I knew he meant it. Leandros loved his family and was very proud of them. He had a lovely wife whom I'd never met and two teenage daughters.

"I'm glad."

"Did you get what I sent?" he asked.

"Yes. Why did you do that? I'm doing okay."

"It's not a present—I'm just finally getting around to sending New Year's gifts to some of my clients. I'm giving each of them an intuitive consultation with you over Skype. They'll be getting in touch with you. They're excited."

Tears of gratitude stung my eyes. "Thank you."

"Stop—it's not a favor. It makes my life so much easier! Besides, I'd like to give them something more helpful than silk ties. I should have thought of it before."

"No, it's perfect timing."

I'd known Leandros since middle school. He grew up poor, raised by a single mother who waitressed at our local diner. His father died when he was three, and he didn't have any other siblings.

We met at the diner: he bussed tables there from the time he was twelve. The first time he saw me, he accidently spilled an entire soda over me—drenching my jeans and sweater. I still smile when I remember that. He prefers to forget it.

He worked hard all through high school and

college, mostly in restaurants, and although he was something of an artist, I knew from early on that he was on a self-directed mission to become a millionaire. It didn't take him all that long. I gave it five years, he did it in three and a half. And he didn't go into the stock market, as so many of our friends did. Instead, he discovered a gift for sales. He went door to door, selling home insurance. His commissions became ridiculously large and he was soon hired by a major insurance company as head of sales. But when he had made his millions, he got bored and decided to go to law school. He worked in Los Angeles for a while, fancying himself a sort of do-gooder Perry Mason, then he got more and more involved in mitigation and insurance issues, and eventually he established his own, very successful law firm.

He was set for life now, even if he never worked again, but Leandros always had to be doing something.

"So what else is going on with you?" he asked. "Everything okay? You're feeling better?"

"Yes, I'm totally recovered. Business is pretty good. Listen to this: Yesterday a client wants me to find his missing daughter. Today I find out he's been murdered."

"What happened to him?"

"He was shot in broad daylight—in a coffee shop. Tons of witnesses."

"Execution-style?"

"Now that you say it, yes, maybe. His name was Joel Wakefield. It's all over the news."

I heard faint tapping on a keyboard and knew he was checking. "Yikes."

"So what do you think?"

"I'm curious… And what about his missing daughter? How old is she?"

"Nineteen. She dropped out of college. He gave me some things to try to find her, receipts, a necklace, a photo. The cops took it all. I'm sure she'll be found now."

He was silent, but I knew he was reading about the murder.

"Leandros?"

"I'm here."

"Do you know anything about Wolcott Candies? There's some connection, but I don't know what it is."

"I'll look into it."

"That would be great."

I heard a phone ringing and voices in the background.

"Gotta go," he said. "My girls are here and we're all heading out. I'll text a list of the gift recipients for the money I sent. Check them off when they call you and let me know how they go."

I heard giggles and then a faint "Are you ready?"

He was probably taking them out for dinner at a fancy restaurant in Malibu, where they live.

"Thanks, Leandros," I said quickly.

I ended the call and poured myself more sparkles.

15. I assumed Percy slept through the night because I didn't hear noises and he didn't text me till nine the next morning.

I brought him coffee and a sort-of Spanish omelet with toast.

"What do we do now?" I asked. "Return the money?"

"First, let's try to find the girl." Percy's mouth was full.

"But what if that detective thinks I'm an accomplice to Joel's murder?"

"You're not."

"But—"

"We'll think about returning the money if you don't find the missing girl, okay? But remember twenty-five percent of that is mine. You can't just give it back without my permission."

I knew he was half-joking, and I wanted that money too, but I also didn't want to be under a cloud of suspicion.

"Well." I finished my toast. "How do we start?"

"Follow the money. Who had access to his account?" Percy began reading off notes from his laptop. "The *Times* says he's divorced. His daughter's mother lives in San Francisco, so maybe that's where she was headed. Her name is Vivian Blum—she kept her maiden name. Their daughter Ruby went to live with her father when she was fifteen. They've been estranged since then. I have a feeling none of them got along."

"I used to live near San Francisco," I said. "Where did Joel Wakefield work? San Francisco too?"

"He moved here five years ago to work with an investment firm on Wall Street."

I was listening with no filters, wondering if just the names he spoke would evoke some insight— whether they'd spark a light. But there was nothing. None of it made any sense.

"I still don't see why she would deposit money in my account. How would an estranged wife know his password, anyway?" I frowned. "His daughter might. But why would she want to?"

"Maybe *she* wants you to find her."

"Why?"

"I don't know…"

"The password issue is big," I pointed out.

"Not really. The most common one is 'password'. Or 'password1'—that's cleverer, people think. Or '1—2—3—4—5—6—7' with minor variations..."

"Really? Somehow I doubt Joel Wakefield is that unsophisticated."

"You might be surprised."

I glanced at him curiously. "Don't tell me you tried it."

Percy looked down at his laptop. "Not rocket science. His was 'qwerty'. That's another classic."

I was excited. "You're kidding me! It worked? What else did you find? Who else has he paid and what deposits has he made? I can't believe you have this information."

"I know, pretty cool."

"Well, *tell me!*"

"There's not much. Three other transactions. Want names?"

"Yes!"

"Tiffany Smithers. John Henry. Wolcott Candies."

"How do we find out about these people?"

"I've done a little research already. Tiffany Smithers is Joel Wakefield's personal assistant. She's worked with him for five years. Lives in Yonkers, likes erotic literature, into BDSM. At least the bondage/discipline aspect of it. She's thirty, a Scorpio, and graduated from Smith."

"How do you *do* this?"

"It's just basic Internet research."

Our eyes met and a funny feeling coursed through me. It wasn't anything like the wild, heady passion I'd had for Leandros practically from the day we met. Nor was it similar to the sturdy tenderness I'd felt for my husband before our divorce. This was a quiet, pink glow in the center of my heart.

I shook myself. He was so young, and anyway he must have a girlfriend—someone important in his life—

"Are your eyes violet?" he asked abruptly.

"Yes."

"It's such a strange color—I've never seen violet eyes before. They're beautiful."

"Thanks." Now my face was pink. "Next?"

"John Henry: forty-five, a Gemini…"

I laughed, but it sounded strained. "Are you

teasing me with these zodiac signs?"

"A little. Want birth dates instead?" He seemed awkward too.

"It doesn't matter. Have your fun. Go on."

"He's Wakefield's half-brother. Lives in Hawai'i. Works in insurance."

"What's the transaction for?"

"Not for business. Says gift. And it's only $900."

"And the company you mentioned?"

"Wolcott Candies: they make candies with flower petals."

"Yum."

I heard Quentin shoveling the snow from the sidewalk, and went outside to give him one of the $100 bills that Leandros had sent me.

"A windfall," I told him, when he refused to take it. "Better accept—you never know when the next one will happen."

He was still reluctant, so I stuffed it into his pocket, and went back inside. Quentin had been a guardian angel to me ever since I'd arrived, and done way more to help me settle than I'd been able to pay him for.

I hadn't told him yet about my leaky ceiling because I knew he'd go up and fix the problem without charging me.

Percy was dozing again, so I went upstairs to work on my sweater, and then I lay down with a book and must have fallen asleep myself. I woke up and saw that it was almost four o'clock.

Time for tea—and I wondered if Percy were awake. I chose a ginger-licorice blend and hoped he would like it. I was a tea junkie. I had over twenty small tins on a shelf, but very little in each because my tea had to be super-fresh for me to enjoy it. There were a few good tea stores in Manhattan, but my favorite was Harney's, and I ordered direct from their factory. I'd learned how to steep the tea so that it was perfect. The water had to be poured just before it boiled or else the leaves lose their flavor. Four minutes was plenty for my favorite oolong.

I always felt there was something magical about tea. Maybe it was because my mother was from England and we always had a ritual of tea at four o'clock when I was growing up. I used to drink it with loads of milk and honey. Now that I'd trained my palate to taste all the varying degrees of flavor in each leaf, I drank it black. Straight. Nothing to taint the delicacy, the deliciousness, the delightfulness.

The water almost boiled and I filled the pot, covered it with a tea cozy, and set it on a tray with two cups.

Percy was still tapping away on his laptop. I set the timer and waited.

He glanced up. "That a bomb?"

"No, a timer."

"What for?"

"So I know when the tea is ready. It can only steep for four minutes."

"Or what will happen?"

"It loses some of its piquancy." We were both more relaxed than we'd been that morning. "Did you find out anything else?"

He turned back to his screen. "So, as I said,

Wakefield's secretary, I mean personal assistant, has a latex fetish."

"Does that have a bearing on the murder?"

"Don't know yet. But it's Saturday night and she's probably going to a fetish party in the East Village."

"How on earth did you find that out?"

"Deductive reasoning. She part-time models for a latex fashionista. Tonight there's a party in the East Village where a new line of clothes will be on show. It's all part of a festival/ birthday/ post-holiday bash. I'm pretty sure she'll be there."

I regarded him doubtfully. "Are you saying I should go?"

"No, I was thinking me."

"But your ankle."

"I know."

I got interested. "I could go, I guess. Try to talk to her. But —"

"What?"

"It's just that on Saturdays I go see a friend of mine. She's ninety, and I shop for her, run errands."

Judy lived in an assisted living facility near the East River. Every week I brought her groceries from the local health food store, and did any other errands she needed. Sometimes we went over her bills and made sure she was up-to-date with them. But most of the time she wanted to talk or we listened to some new meditative music I brought her. Sometimes we did gentle yoga stretches together.

At the same time, I knew that of all my friends, Judy would be one who would understand why I had to cancel our standing appointment. If she needed something urgently, I could always pop over there in the middle of the week.

Percy was shaking his head. "Anyway, I think you definitely should *not* go to the latex party."

I looked at him curiously. "Why not? Too dangerous?"

16. "The party's harmless, in a painful kind of way. More worried about you."

"Me? Why?"

He regarded me so warmly I thought he was going to say something nice about how I looked, but he said, "You're connected to Joel Wakefield's murder. Better stay home."

I was touched by his concern, but by this time I was excited at the idea of going out. I wanted to be *doing* something. It wasn't just about venturing into a fetish party—something I'd never done before—but the idea of meeting Joel Wakefield's personal assistant. I was sure I would find a clue somehow that would help me find out who murdered Joel Wakefield and why. More importantly, I wanted to find out who deposited the $5,000 into my account after he was dead. Might it have been her?

And, best case scenario, maybe she had an idea about Ruby's whereabouts.

As I knew she would be, Judy was happy to postpone our meeting for a week. She assured me she had everything she needed, and would be glad to hear about my adventures whenever I had time.

Since I'd never owned a piece of latex clothing in my life, I dressed in satin leggings, black and sleek, a sequined halter top, and a black cashmere cardigan. I paid particular attention to outlining my violet eyes, seeing them differently because of Percy's earlier comment. My face was narrow, the eyebrows dark, my skin pale. I had a real nose and my teeth were never straightened, so they had some personality. But I'd found that when you reached a certain age—mine was late forties—it was hard to know what you really looked like. Sometimes I'd imagine myself as I used to look, and at other times as I felt inside. When I was still fragile from a bad case of influenza, that wasn't all great.

But tonight I saw myself through Percy's eyes and I felt as shimmery as the sparkling wine I sipped as I got ready. The velvet and silver gloves Brigitte had given me the night before matched my outfit perfectly. My vegan boots looked shiny and spiky.

When Percy saw me his eyes widened and he looked like he might choke on his tea.

"Think they'll let me in?" I asked.

"They'll want twelve of you."

My gold-lined cloak hung on the hook by the front door. I put it on, and pulled up the velvet hood so it framed my face.

"Need a broomstick to get there?" Percy teased.

"Haha." I smiled.

My cloak was not at all like a witch's cloak. It was made of fine Melton wool, which made it rain- and snow-resistant and it was incredibly warm. The graceful hood was lined with dark gold velvet, and fell down my back in lovely folds when I didn't have it up.

Percy still looked worried. "You'll be careful, won't you? Take a cab there and back."

I smiled reassuringly at him. "Yes, I will. Don't worry about me."

"Have an extra set of keys for your house?" he asked.

"Why? You're not going anywhere."

"Well, if I have to. You know, like if something happens."

I remembered again that I hardly knew this guy. Maybe this entire episode was some elaborate scam and I was going to be robbed blind. Maybe that look he gave me was just pretend.

But in my heart I was sure I could trust him.

"There's a spare set in that bowl by the front door. But don't go anywhere. Let the ankle get better so you can get that cast put on first thing Monday."

17. I set out into the cold. It was no longer snowing, but there was snow piled everywhere from yesterday's storm. It seemed almost pretty, as long as you didn't have to climb through it.

It was still early enough for there to be plenty of taxis cruising Sixth Avenue, and I settled on the back seat of one for the short drive, trying not to be too jumpy about what I might be getting into.

The place in alphabet town was sleek and sophisticated in a funky East Village sort of way. The cab let me off in front of a four-story loft building and I rang the doorbell. Someone must have approved of my appearance, because the metal door swung open and I was ushered inside a fur-lined hallway by a strong-looking bouncer with no hair and a gentle smile. He took my cloak and then sent me along the hall alone.

Sure I was skittish. I had vague ideas of BDSM types of scenarios playing out in front of me, and perhaps some pressure to partake in dungeon games.

But the reality was quiet and dignified. The hall opened into a large room with a deep red carpet and soft purple and yellow vinyl sofas. The drapes in the tall windows were made of real teal latex. People stood around, chatting conversationally despite their flamboyant get-ups, most of which, by the way, were not nearly as kinky or weird as I imagined they would be. I saw nightclub sophisticates, military get-ups, velvet ball gowns, and latex—latex—latex.

I definitely felt underdressed and wished I'd worn my lace bustier instead of the sequined tank, and done my hair with my jeweled combs.

I surveyed the room. A six-foot, dark-haired beauty in a gold lamé tight-fitting gown and matching gold sandals scrutinized me with dark, come-hither eyes that sent a little shiver up the backs of my legs. Before anything else could happen, though, a cute blond man in a throat-to-toe black latex jumpsuit approached, holding two glasses. He handed me one.

"Champagne?"

"You read my mind." I smiled at him. "Thank you."

The champagne was real. A nice treat.

"First time?" he asked.

"Is it obvious?"

"Only to some of us. I'm from London and fetish clubs are more common there. You Americans are still Puritans at heart."

"In a way, yes we are," I agreed. "I'm Sati. So what do I need to know?"

"Do you like to dance?"

"Love to."

"So we'll start there. Then you'll have another glass of champagne and I'll show you around. You might not want to check out the dungeon your first time here. But we'll see."

He was so cheerful and fresh-faced that I felt comfortable right away. He led me by my gloved hand to the adjoining room, where disco balls and laser beams twinkled and glowed on a gleaming dance floor. It wasn't over-crowded; I had arrived pretty early—it wasn't midnight yet.

All kinds of people were dancing, twenty-year-olds, middle-aged people, and there was one man in full latex tuxedo who must have been at least eighty.

Some of the dancers were in black Goth. Still others were bikini-clad. Most looked as glamorous as if they'd stepped out of a Saks Fifth Avenue window around holiday season. But I also saw collars around necks, and delicate chains dangling provocatively from under bustieres. The shoes were the most impressive to me: from stilettos to latex boots that made the wearer look like a super hero, to someone with a pair of sandals made of metal mesh. Mostly there was the latex that smoothed all the bulges and crinkles in their bodies to exquisite sensuality.

The music was throbbing and erotic. My London friend bobbed good-naturedly while we chatted.

"What do you do?" he asked.

"I'm an intuitive consultant."

He raised an eyebrow and immediately held out his hand, palm up, still bobbing up and down to the music. "Do you read palms?"

I laughed. "I'll give you my card."

The music changed to something slower and he took me in his arms, his smooth latex pressed against my silk. I was starting to enjoy dancing together, but then the image of Percy's encouraging grin surfaced and I reminded myself why I was there.

"I'm supposed to meet someone here. Her name's Tiffany. Know her?"

"Tiffany? Yes, she's here. And I think you're ready for that second champagne. Come on, I'll help you find her."

We returned to the sumptuous lounge where the bar was located. The bartender, naked except for a royal blue latex apron, served us politely. On a plush couch, a man was using his riding crop to tenderly strike a woman who was crouched on her knees, her butt raised high in the air. He finished after just a few strokes, and kissed the back of her neck. She wore a pretty, fur-lined collar.

"Ah, here she is," said my London friend, who was a few steps ahead of me. I hoped no one had caught me staring. "Tiffany, there's someone here who wants to meet you. This is Sati."

Tiffany turned out to be one of the dancers wearing a red latex bikini. She was busty and toned and looked like she worked out in her sleep. Her eyes were bright blue and curious and her round face was surrounded by curls.

We shook hands.

"Welcome. First time?" Her voice was little-girl and husky.

London met my eyes with a grin and drifted away.

"It is," I smiled at her. "But how can you tell? Is there a special handshake or something?"

She gurgled throatily. "Not at all. It's a look newcomers have. It's awesome. Did you get something to eat? I'm starved."

It turned out there was a lavish buffet in an adjoining room, with small café tables, some of which were occupied and some not. It was all so quiet and elegant that it was hard to imagine what might be happening in the dungeons below. We helped ourselves to curry and poppadums and sat at one of the tables. Another naked waiter in a blue latex apron brought over a glass of champagne and put it in front of me.

"Would you like one too?" he asked Tiffany.

"No thanks—I've already spent my budget for tonight."

"Is this going on some mysterious bill?" I asked. "I haven't paid for any drinks yet."

The waiter answered; "First timers get the first two glasses free. After that they're eight dollars a class."

"I'll treat you," I said to Tiffany.

"Wow—thanks."

When the waiter brought the second glass, we dug into the fragrant curry.

"So why did you want to meet me?" Tiffany asked, gulping down the bubbles. "Mutual friend?"

"Not exactly. I knew your boss, Joel Wakefield. Tiffany, I'm so sorry about what happened to him."

18. Right away I could tell she did not like this topic of conversation at all. She refused to look at me and obviously didn't know what to say.

"I guess you're wondering why I'm partying," she said at last. Her voice was darker than it had been.

"Not at all. Look, I'm here too. I'm just trying to find out something about him. He paid me to find his missing daughter. I'm wondering if you could help."

"No, I can't." She looked so distressed I was afraid she might cry.

I reassured her. "It's just that the police think I'm involved in some kind of scam and I'm not. I thought you could help me, maybe tell the cops that I never met your boss before he came to see me last Thursday." She still didn't look at me, so I continued, "I don't mean to upset you. I totally understand if you don't want to get involved."

She didn't respond, and eventually she went back to her champagne, which she finished, and then pushed away the rest of her curry. I wondered how I was going to report this conversation to Percy. I knew he expected more from me.

"Maybe I could come to your office on Monday, and you would talk to me then?" I asked.

Vigorously, she shook her curls. "I don't know anything. All I did was keep appointments, answer his phone, make travel arrangements. That's absolutely all. I can't help you. Besides, I might not even have a job after Monday."

"Is there anyone in the office who could help me? Someone who had access to his personal bank account?"

"*No!*" Now she sounded almost frantic. "There's no one—*no one.* He took care of all his personal banking himself!" She stood up hastily and wiped her hands on the shiny red bikini bottom. Her nude stockinged legs were gorgeous and on her feet were pretty black suede bootlets. "I really wish I could help you," and this time she was looking right at me and I knew she meant it. "I really do. But I can't. I know you'll be all right, though. I'm going to miss Joel very much. He was a good boss."

She backed away toward the dance floor.

Time to leave. Retrieving my cloak from the bouncer, I said goodnight and left. Outside the cold winter night air ripped through my cloak as I clutched it tightly around me. There was a cab on the far side of the street, but the fare light was off. As fast as I could, I clip-clopped on my spiky heels toward First Avenue.

I hadn't gone half way down the block when I got that light inside me that happened sometimes—but this time it was a warning light.

Something was wrong.

Hurry.

Before I could even begin to respond, a stocky man with menacing eyes and a very short beard appeared in front of me as if from nowhere. I startled, then walked around him and kept going, trying to ignore the light inside me that urged me to run.

The man jumped in front of me, thrusted close, and pointed a small, evil-looking gun straight at my heart.

I almost peed in my satin leggings. "Do you want my purse?" I gasped, completely forgetting about using my Voice. "Or my wallet? I have some cash."

He snarled something that I did not understand, probably because I was in shock. The shoulder strap of my purse was around my neck, underneath my cloak, so I couldn't take it off and hand it to him.

Instead I opened it with trembling fingers and took out my wallet.

With his gun, he knocked the wallet to the pavement and barked something about five thousand dollars.

"What?" I said, thinking I didn't hear correctly.

The gun pressed into my ribcage again and I gasped in pain, afraid I was going to pass out.

Just then I heard the pounding of running feet behind me. The man looked past my shoulder and my numbed senses started to return. I knew what I had to do. While his eyes were focused on my oncoming rescuer, I delivered a sharp karate blow to the gun. It clattered to the pavement and slid into the gutter by the wheels of a parked car.

The next thing I saw was a fist slamming into the man's bearded jaw. He staggered back, clutching his face, moaning and whining.

My rescuer turned to me and grabbed my hands in his.

"Are you okay?"

I gasped.

"Percy!"

19. The bearded stranger lurched down the street and disappeared into the dark. Neither of us bothered to chase after him. Limping badly, Percy picked up my wallet, handed it to me, and ushered me toward the dark cab still parked across from the party. The driver came toward us, cell phone to his ear, hopefully calling the police.

"You all right, ma'am?" he asked.

I nodded, barely. Percy bundled me into the back seat, and we sat there in the dark as the sirens neared.

I was breathing hard. "What about your leg?" I said at last. "Isn't it broken?"

"That's all you can think of?" He was angry, but I could see it was from fear. Afraid for me. He was *afraid* for me.

Why?

"What's going on?" I demanded, but more calmly.

"I was worried about you."

"I meant, your ankle. It's not hurt?"

"What? Of course it is!" He looked so concerned, his eyes wide, that I calmed down. Besides, didn't he just save my life?

Maybe.

But what if he and the mugger were involved in some bizarre con together?

No, that was ridiculous. I had no money. I was being paranoid.

"How can you run with a broken ankle?" I asked.

"It's a fracture, not a break, and football players do it all the time," he replied grimly. "And it hurts like hell."

"I'm sorry. Then—thank you. But why are you

here? What happened?"

"Someone came looking for you earlier." His voice was raised above the yowl of oncoming sirens. "He knocked on your door and I answered. I guess I shouldn't have, but I didn't think about it. Anyway, it was some guy who threatened you—and me. He said he wanted that $5,000. I slammed the door in his face, but I got nervous when you didn't answer your phone, and came after you. The bouncer wouldn't let me inside 'cos I wasn't dressed well enough. So I waited for you."

"And … the mugger—he's the same man who came to my house?"

"Yep."

I took out my phone, checked the myriad urgent text messages from Percy, took a deep breath. "I had the volume turned off. Thank you."

The driver was silent. He didn't speak English very well, but we all three got out of the taxi to tell the police what happened.

At least, we told them most of what happened. I didn't mention that he'd demanded $5,000 from me. It seemed ludicrous and unless we went into the whole story of Joel's PayPal transaction, it wouldn't make any sense.

Percy leaned on his crutches, his face drawn. I told the cops that his ankle was broken and finally they let him sit on the back seat of the taxi while they continued to question us. There were two of them.

Eventually, they said they had enough information and they'd try to follow up. I doubted they'd ever find the mugger, and I could see they were doubtful too, but it was nice of them to pretend to try.

The driver had left the meter running the entire time and by the time we turn onto Gay Street we owed him $45. I handed him three twenties, while Percy, using his crutches, climbed the five steep steps to the front door. He refused my help. His wounded leg was bare except for the bandage. It was definitely swollen and he was cringing with every step.

I stuck the key into the lock and he clutched the rail, standing on one foot. The cab drove away.

We went inside and the door swung closed behind us.

"Need help getting settled?" I asked uncertainly.

He shook his head and went into his room without saying goodnight.

I was too tired to do anything but put on cozy sweatpants and a soft, long-sleeved top and climb into my couch-bed. Weird images of shiny latex, polite conversation, gentle spankings, vibrant pink, orange, green, and festive light decorations circled like a kaleidoscope in my head as I fell asleep.

20. I awoke on Sunday morning more determined than ever to try to find Joel Wakefield's daughter. That felt more urgent than following the perplexing PayPal transaction, or figuring out who pulled the trigger. It was as though Joel Wakefield had charged me with a task of vital significance.

I hoped with all my heart Ruby had not encountered the bearded hostile mugger I'd had to deal with the night before.

Tying the sash of my dark green velvet robe around my waist, I went downstairs to the kitchen for coffee. I hoped Percy was still asleep—he deserved some good rest.

Limping after me like that on a fractured ankle…what an idiot he was! And what friend he was turning out to be!

For a moment, I considered telling him he could stay longer, after his cast was put on, and while his ankle healed, but if he camped in the office, where would I read for my clients?

Tomorrow was Monday, and I had someone scheduled for noon. I could bring them upstairs and read at the table here. I looked around, trying to decide whether a reading in my kitchen area was a good idea or not.

I made toast, boiled an egg, opened my laptop.

There were a few emails I needed to answer, including three from clients of Leandros who wanted to schedule readings. Leandros—my personal Lorenzo de' Medici.

I heard hopping downstairs—Percy was awake. I ground some fresh coffee and made him a cup, popped bread in the toaster, and scrambled some eggs. It was sunny today, and the kitchen was bright.

Downstairs, Percy was sitting up on the couch.

He looked glad to see me.

"Coffee?" I greeted him. "Hungry?"

"Yep."

I put the tray on his lap. "Thanks, Percy. I mean for last night. Coming out after me like that—I'm really grateful."

He didn't look at me, but at his plate. I could tell he was embarrassed. His phone buzzed and he reached for it. He seemed to get even more self-conscious as he texted back, hastily. From the way he was hunched over, and his expression, I knew he was texting a woman.

"Everything okay?" I asked when he set down the phone and turned back to his eggs.

He nodded. "Just trying to make arrangements for tomorrow, after I get the cast on. I'm going to need help climbing those stairs to my apartment. A friend said I could stay at her place, but she lives in Hoboken, and I'm not going to be ready for subway stairs yet. She's looking into a car service."

I wondered about his 'friend'—whether or not they were romantically involved. But if so, why hadn't she come to visit him?

Funny, how possessive I was starting to feel about him.

"How are you going to help me find Ruby if you're in Hoboken? And what about all those clients you said you'd find me? Can you do it all online?"

"Oh, sure."

"Because I was thinking of setting up an office for you in the front room—turn it into a reception area. Give you a place to work."

Looking interested, he picked up his crutches and went into the front room. I followed him, coffee cup in hand. There was a hardback chair, a hook by the front door with my cloak hanging on it, but very little else. I hadn't paid a lot of attention to this area before. It felt more of a vestibule than a place to embellish.

I'd never actually had anyone wait in here; they always come straight in for their reading. Now, with Percy looking around the room, I saw it differently. For one thing, it was much larger than I realized. It would be easy to put a reception desk by the window, so that when someone entered they'd be greeted by a real person instead of a blank, beige wall.

"See, there's plenty of room for a desk over there," I pointed.

He nodded. "And that way I could make sure you get paid before you give your consultation."

"So even if they don't like what I tell them…"

We both laughed.

"Have a desk?" he asked. "Or an extra chair?"

"No, but my friend Brigitte has furniture in storage that she's been trying to give me. I'll ask her."

"And the room where you do your consults needs more personality. To reflect you."

"Yes, I've been meaning to do that too," I said. "It just wasn't the right time before now."

"You don't need a lot. Simple and stylish."

"Yes, I agree. Brigitte says exactly the same thing."

"Why don't you call your friend and see what she has?"

"You mean right now?"

"Why not?"

21. We were definitely in some kind of a flow, because within three hours Brigitte showed up with two large men-friends and a pick-up truck filled with treasures. First they brought in two distinctive scissor chairs and a matching ottoman, upholstered in antique rose velvet.

I couldn't resist sitting in one of the chairs and immediately decided never to get up again. "Oh, how gorgeous. But I can't take these. Aren't they Ward Bennett?"

"Oh, they were in storage," Brigitte shrugged nonchalantly. "They belonged to my parents. I knew I would find a home for them one day."

Their rosiness jumped out against the cream-and-coffee walls. Brigitte was so excited that I was finally paying attention to the interior design of my house that I hardly had to do anything.

She also flirted intensely with Percy, under the guise of decorating for me, that it left very little space for me to take part in the design process. Percy, it turned out, was a flirt himself.

A sleek, simple desk was brought in next and placed where Percy pointed. Then there was an emerald tufted adjustable desk chair, floating like a throne above a walnut cruciform base. He sat in it, and it was as though he belonged.

Even though Brigitte's blatant attraction to Percy annoyed me, I had to admit the room was starting to look great. The pure lines and fine fabrics were offset by the warm open bricks of one wall and the simple linen drapes in the tall windows.

"You need a little bell on the desk," Brigitte said. "Your Percy can ring it a few minutes before your session is up. I know for a fact you go way over time with your clients."

"That's a good idea," Percy said. "That way you won't get behind schedule."

Since I hadn't had more than one or two clients in a single day, I thought that was sweet of them.

"I don't have a bell, but I have a singing bowl," I suggested. "Could you use that?"

"Perfect," said Brigitte, and when I brought it out of the oak chest where I'd stored it, she proceeded to try to show Percy how to use it.

When her friends brought in a few rolled up Oriental rugs, she dismissed them. "Those old things! They have holes."

More for something to do than because I wanted holey carpets, I cut the string that tied one of them and discovered a substantial Bidjar. It had an ivory diamond-shaped medallion in its center, surrounded by indigo and crimson flowers and vines. There were no holes that I could see.

"Are you sure you don't want it?" I asked Brigitte in amazement.

But she definitely had other ideas for her own apartment, which was mostly glass and chrome. She waved away all the rugs. "They're yours, darling. Now, what about your consult room? That's of equal importance. Lowell!" Imperiously gesturing one of the men, she instructed him to bring in the rest of the furniture. There was a button-tufted settee for my clients to sit on, but the piece-de-resistance, for me anyway, was the burnt-orange velour chair they all agreed would be my 'reading' chair. It was large as a throne, but it was on wheels and actually swiveled.

"I love it," I said.

"The drapes you have are okay—I like the chocolate color," approved Brigitte. They had been there when I'd moved in. "Velvet is always chic. But that painting has to go."

We all looked over at the mantel. A painting Leandros made when he was still in college hung on the exposed brick wall over the fireplace. It was mostly abstract colors, but because I knew it so well, I could make out a gray-and-pumpkin lighthouse on a windswept, rocky coast.

He'd painted it from his imagination, so it wasn't relevant to some place we both knew or anything like that. I hung it there not only because he gave it to me, as a keepsake, but also because it's become one of my favorite images for the Tower. I am one of those few people who really likes the Tower when it shows up in a tarot spread. It gives me a pleasant shiver of excitement. It means something is definitely over—

finished—and can finally be discarded. There is space for the new.

Leandros's version of the Tower was dark and murky, and the waves lashing at the foundation of the lighthouse were tearing it away. Sometimes I even could make out people tumbling into the churning sea, although at other times they were rocks. There was lightning coming down, penetrating the granite sky, which had been cracked open and shattered.

Sometimes when I looked at the painting, I wished Leandros still painted.

"But it looks good there," I protested.

"But it doesn't match," Brigitte argued.

Percy had gone close to it, and was studying it carefully, leaning on his crutches. He didn't say anything.

Brigitte gave up the argument and turned back to the middle of the room, where her two friends were placing the low oak chest in the center of the carpet.

"You need a coffee table to do your readings on," she said. "Maybe we can go shopping all together."

But I liked the chest I used. Inside it I kept crystals, decks of cards, incense, things like that, and it was just the right height for my readings.

She let me leave the simple clock on the wall too, which was good, since I needed it there. By this time it was already six and early wintry night had long since fallen. I drew the chocolate velvet drapes that now looked rich and tasty with the splashes of orange and emerald to offset them.

"Where's the old couch gonna go?" asked one of the menfriends from the front room. They had moved it out of the office and now it was propped up by the front door. "Into storage? The armchair, too?"

Brigitte wrinkled her nose. "On the street. Someone will appreciate them."

I looked at Percy. He looked back. I knew we were both thinking the same thing.

"Basement?" I said out load.

22.

Brigitte gave an excited squeal. "Of course! A new tenant! How perfect!"

"Wait a moment," Percy said quickly, watching me.

"Yes, wait." I had to think. Wasn't he getting much too knotted up in my life very fast? We'd already committed to a temporary business partnership, but did I want him to actually live in my house? I felt our lives were already becoming too entangled.

For all Brigitte's pushiness, she could be hyper-sensitive. "Just till the ankle is better," she demurred persuasively. "Why not? There's no one there now. And that will give us a place to put the old furniture."

I knew it made sense. I hated the thought of

Percy climbing up five flights on his crutches. Or hanging out in some mythical apartment in Hoboken.

But I was nervous. Too much had happened, too fast.

I remembered the lenormand spread I'd done it seemed like years ago: the Rider right over the House. Had that meant that Percy would move into my basement apartment?

Everyone was looking at me, wondering why I hesitated.

"Okay," I said.

"I'll keep my apartment in Coney Island and move back there end of February," Percy said. "And I'll pay you up front for two months. It'll come out of my disability check."

Brigitte beamed as though she was making a huge commission as a realtor and we all went out the back door, through the pocket garden, and into the basement apartment.

It was really cozy, with a living room and kitchen appliances in the front and a tiny bedroom in the back which opened onto the garden. There was a Murphy bed in there which still worked fine.

The windows in the front were at street level and we could see the boots of passers-by crunching in the snow.

I could tell Percy really liked it down here. In fact, I hadn't realized before how cute it was, but seeing it through his eyes, especially after he'd been sleeping on a lumpy couch in an office for three nights, I could see the appeal. Brigitte's beefy men brought down the sofa so Percy had something to sit on besides the window ledge. Even Percy vetoed the armchair, though, and they left it on the sidewalk at the end of Gay Street.

Brigitte tried to get us to go out to a restaurant, but Percy looked pretty tired, so I declined for us both. I promised her we'd go out soon, and thanked her again for the furniture.

She gave me a hug. "I'm so glad it's finally out of storage," she said. "Now I have room to put my other crap in there."

They left. I didn't know how I'd ever be able to repay her, but I figured that would come in time.

Percy lay down on the couch while I went upstairs to get him a set of sheets and a blanket, and a couple of towels.

As I made his bed, I called to him, "Where did you grow up?"

"In the city."

"Where?"

"Upper West Side. My parents worked at the New York Times. I always thought I'd be a journalist. Jimmy Olsen was my hero."

"So why aren't you?" I asked.

"It's all different now. I wanted to be out in the field, doing things, finding out things, talking to people. But now that's almost all done online."

"Why UPS?"

"At first it was for the money. Student loans, mostly. And I worked during holidays and summers. But then I got sucked in. Thought it might be a career track."

"It still might be."

He didn't respond. He had been working all morning on setting up social media accounts for me, writing blurbs that made me blush, and he even put together a website where people could contact me. We found a photo of me from a few years ago when I was at the top of the Empire State building looking out over the city. It was a nice shot—Leandros had taken it and I had that spellbound look that works well in photographs.

Percy was still tapping keys when I finished making his bed.

"What are you doing there?" I asked.

He looked up. "Trying to figure out who else had access to Wakefield's PayPal account and could have transferred that $5,000. You've ruled out his secretary, right?"

"Yeah, I'm sure she has nothing to do with it."

He looked at me curiously. "Can you really tell just from looking at someone if they're guilty, lying, hiding something?"

That was not an easy question to answer. "It's not that I say to myself, this lady is guilty. It's more of a feeling. I can feel when something is off. It's like a note that's off-key. Then I have to look more closely and figure out why. And I also have to clear any reaction I might have from my own issues. It's complicated."

Since he was still regarding me, I went on: "It's not something I can take credit for. It's just something that happens." He nodded slowly, still gazing at me. I steered the conversation back to our investigation.

"What else have you found out? Who were the other two people you mentioned earlier?"

"John Henry: forty-five years old … He's Wakefield's half-brother. Lives in Hawai'i. Works in insurance."

"And the company you mentioned?"

"Wolcott: they make candies with flower petals."

"That's right. But why would someone from a candy company send me $5,000? Why would Joel Wakefield's half-brother? I don't get it. Not just that, I don't get how we would find out."

He nodded, but didn't seem daunted. "Do you like jigsaw puzzles?"

"Sometimes. I don't do them often, though. I have a friend I play chess with whenever we get together."

"Chess is good too. But I like puzzles better. When you're trying to figure something out, first you create the frame with the straight edges. You make piles of color here and there. And then the pieces start falling into place."

I liked that analogy. "I get it."

"But in the beginning, it's just a big pile of cardboard bits."

I realized we were gazing at each other again, as though we'd known each other for a long time but had only recently encountered each other again.

23. I decided it was time to tell Percy about Leandros. Before going to work together for the next six weeks or so it would be best if he knew that Leandros was part of my life, and always would be, in spite of the fact that we were no longer together. And it wasn't even that I saw him all that often, but he called at least once a week, we Skyped fairly often, and he was always somewhere on my mind.

"I have a friend," I said. "His name is Leandros. He lives in Los Angeles. We've known each other forever. We grew up together."

Percy's eyes were back on the screen but his fingers were still.

For some reason I couldn't go on with what I was going to say. Instead I said, "Leandros might be able to find out something about John Henry. He's a lawyer and he's pretty good at finding stuff about people. Or he has a staff that does, anyway."

"Good," Percy said. "I'll send you what we know about him so far and you can forward it to him."

"Do you think I could get into trouble simply because someone transferred that money into my account?" I asked. "Will the cops come back and arrest me?"

"Ask your lawyer-friend," Percy advised. "What does he think?"

I texted that question about my being arrested to Leandros and he responded right away. *"Let them try!*

Don't worry—I'm here for you."

Percy saw me smiling at the text. "Guess he thinks you're safe?"

I nodded, but didn't read the text out loud. Instead I texted Leandros back: *Want to help find out about a possible suspect?*

I knew he'd say yes. Within a few minutes, Percy had sent me personal stuff about John Henry, and I forwarded it to Leandros: *"John Henry: forty-five years old. Lives in Kailua, divorced. VP for an insurance company. Relationship with Joel Wakefield: Same mother, different father. One son, still in high school, lives with mom."*

Any information Leandros or one of his many minions could muster would be helpful. And since I already gave him an outline of what had happened, I knew he'd be intrigued.

"Okay—and what about Wolcott Candies?" I asked Percy next. "What's that connection?"

Percy looked frustrated. "I can't come up with anything. It's a boutique candy-maker, originally based out of a small town south of Boston, but it's become a huge corporation over the past ten years. Their sweets have become pretty popular... but maybe Joel just ordered a box for a friend. Maybe we're making more of those transactions than we should."

While we pondered how to dig out the relationship between Wolcott Candies and Joel Wakefield, I ordered pizza to be delivered.

Then I got a few sheets of blank white paper and cut them into small rectangles.

"What are you doing?" he asked.

"I liked your analogy of a picture puzzle," I said. "I'm going to see if this helps."

When I finished cutting the squares, Percy helped me color-coordinate them.

"Missing daughter: make those blue. Joel Wakefield in red, since he's the murder victim. PayPal transaction—green."

I used sharpies and began. In the "missing daughter" pile there were the clues Joel had left with me that were now in the possession of the police.

In green we had John Henry, Wolcott Candies, and Tiffany.

In red we had very little.

"Anything else?" I asked.

"Yep. The most important thing."

"What's that?"

"You."

"What about me?"

"Why did Joel Wakefield come to you?"

I felt a little offended. "Because I'm good at what I do."

"You say yourself you're not psychic in the way he was asking you to be. Why wouldn't he call one of those one-800 psychic people then?"

"What're you saying?"

"I think he chose you for a reason. You're sure you never met him before?"

I shook my head. "Positive."

"There's gotta be a connection."

"Why?"

"Because if there wasn't, that $5,000 wouldn't be

in your PayPal account."

"A friend referred him to me." I hesitated. "This friend really liked me—sort of had a crush, I guess. So he probably exaggerated how wonderful I was."

"I doubt he exaggerated. But I still think there's another reason he chose you."

"It's possible someone knew he'd come to see me. Maybe there was something about the appointment in his calendar. And the murderer thought it would be smart to use me as a cover. A frame?"

"Let's look at the timing of what happened," Percy said. "Wakefield came to see you on Thursday at 11 a.m. He left at noon, without paying."

"That's right."

"Okay. The next morning we sent him an invoice through PayPal. I did that around nine. He paid it practically immediately. We invoiced him for the $5,000, at 11, an hour after he was murdered."

"Then he paid me four hours after he was murdered."

"I didn't see the transaction till three-thirty, but, yes, it went through at two. Then the cops arrived."

"Then there was the party in the East Village and that guy accosted me, threatening to kill me if I didn't return his $5,000. Who the heck was he?" I gazed down at the white rectangles of paper. "Where do I put that piece—the bearded guy? What color?"

"Yellow—unknown." Percy frowned. "I wonder if Wakefield's daughter has shown up yet."

"Can you find out?"

Percy tapped some keys. "Might be on the news," he said. "The funeral's tomorrow—there might be some info. I'll check."

I waited, looking at cards in front of me, letting them blur together. I moved them around. Twitched them. Replaced one with another.

"According to latest news reports, his daughter is still missing." Percy's voice sounded far away.

"Hm."

I rearranged the cards in blue. The Greyhound bus. The receipt from the coffee shop. The candy wrapper.

The old photograph. She was a pretty girl, with reddish hair.

I imagined her huddled in a bus station, fending off drunken leers and groping hands.

But somehow that wasn't it. Instead I saw her in a sea of people—crowds and crowds of them. They were all making strange noises, but I couldn't tell what they were.

I felt very far away and reached for another card to draw myself back to the little house on Gay Street.

I picked it up. The receipt for the bus ticket to San Francisco.

24. I looked at Percy. "That money's still in my account, right? It hasn't been frozen or anything?"

"Yep."

"I think it's time to use some of it for expenses. I need to take a trip."

He glanced at the piece of paper in my hand. "San Francisco. Since you lived there, you'll know what to do."

"What do you mean?"

"You'd know the places to go—where she might be hiding ..."

"I'm not sure about that. I never really got to know the city. I was at school there, stayed mostly on campus."

"Probably know it better than you think."

"Do you really think that's where she is?"

"There's that bus receipt. Also, her mother lives there. She grew up there."

"I don't see how I could find her if the cops can't, though."

"Maybe not," he said, "but you could try. You have a credit card, don't you?"

I did, but I rarely used it. I preferred cash—it made every transaction feel more real and tangible. Using a credit card made me feel like I was paying for something twice, which made it seem twice as expensive.

But now was a time to use my credit card, I knew that.

"I'll find you a flight. Tomorrow?"

I fished the card out of my wallet and handed it to Percy.

"Early as possible," I said. "I'll cancel tomorrow's appointment."

"I'll take care of it."

While I waited, I went upstairs, showered, and got ready for bed. I had a feeling tomorrow was going to be a busy day. Snugly wrapped in my green robe, I went back out through the freezing cold garden into his apartment.

"Any luck?"

"Yep. You're booked on a flight at nine tomorrow morning. You'll be in San Francisco by noon. Now all you have to do is pack. You'll be gone two days. Think that's enough time?"

"To find her? I have no idea."

"I think you'll find her."

"Where will I stay?"

"I got a pretty decent rate at a hotel near the airport."

"What do I do when I get there?" I ask.

"You'll know," he assured me. "Maybe there are homeless shelters you could check out. Youth hostels. I'll check into people she might know there—school friends, for example."

"How can you do that?"

"Facebook? I'll see what I can come up with."

We looked at each other.

"You're getting the cast on tomorrow," I remembered. "Are you going to be okay by yourself?"

"Of course. I have friends." He held out the silver pendant that belonged to Ruby. "Take this with you. I have a feeling it'll keep you on course."

25.

I've never met anyone who doesn't love San Francisco. Not only Tony Bennett, but everyone does. And I don't blame them. San Francisco is small, clean, sweet, dramatic, romantic, sophisticated, historical. Ocean, mountain, skyscrapers, Chinatown, stunning bridges galore, and yummy food.

But I wasn't one of them. I'd gone there to pursue a graduate degree soon after I'd heard Leandros had gotten married. Remembering those years I lived there, when I'd been at a low point, I felt unexcited about the trip. I had not been back since then and, in spite of Percy's confidence in me, I felt out of my depth.

During the flight, I tried to strategize a way to find Ruby—something the police might not have thought of. I scrolled through texts Percy had sent earlier, suggesting people and places I could explore while I was here. A list of homeless shelters, three youth hostels, names of people Ruby grew up with or was connected to through Facebook. There was more than a week's worth of intense searching if I were to follow up on all these leads.

But I knew the police had already checked out all those places and people. All standard.

And I was pretty sure they were on the wrong track, but I didn't know why.

Ruby's ticket—the one from two weeks ago—had been for a bus. But one year ago, Percy had discovered, she had flown into the San Francisco airport. He had pointed out that the withdrawals from her bank account had started a year ago as well.

Coincidence?

I don't believe in those things.

I had a strong feeling that my search needed to start at the airport. But when the plane landed, I still had no idea how to begin.

Tote in hand, my cloak flowing behind me, I headed toward the airport exit.

Then I paused.

Begin where you are.

When Ruby had gotten off the plane, something had happened to her here. Something that was connected to the $50 withdrawals from her bank account.

But what?

I paused, sat on a chair near baggage claim, and looked around. I was surrounded by the usual bustle-and-boredom mood of an airport. A small child fell over near me, and her bottle rolled under my chair. I picked her up and handed her the bottle, magically transforming a loud wail into a sunny smile.

A little later, a nice-looking gentleman approached, offering to take me out for coffee. I declined. My neighbor, an English tourist, began chatting with me, so I moved to a bench closer to the exit. I needed to focus. I didn't know what I was waiting for, but the longer I was there, the more certain I became that I needed to wait.

An hour passed, then two. I texted Percy, telling

him where I was, but he didn't respond.

I closed my eyes, doubting myself all over again. I heard no message. I felt no fluid light filling me with confidence and certainty, the way it used to. There was just…nothing.

Very disheartening.

But I went on waiting.

After a while, I hopelessly gave up trying to be intuitive and instead opened my eyes again.

I longed for my intuition to come back to me with a fierceness that made me want to stamp my foot in rage. Ruby needed me—and here I was, stuck in an airport terminal, with no sense of where to go, what to do.

Two middle-aged women were approaching me. They were dressed conservatively in skirts, nylons, walking shoes. One of them held a leaflet.

When I was growing up the Hare Krishna people and Jews for Jesus were always handing me leaflets at airports. Not anymore, though. Not since 9/11. Nowadays, airport security frowned on soliciting.

These women looked remarkably nondescript— no orange gowns or loud drums, as I remembered from travel in my youth. No briefcases, like the Jehovah's Witnesses usually had, filled with pamphlets. They almost looked unsure of themselves, as though I might start shouting for help any minute.

Maybe that had happened to them before.

I felt something well up inside me. Time to pay attention. *Notice*.

The women glanced surreptitiously around

before approaching me. Then they came over.

"Hello," one of them said.

The other one—who was timidly holding the flyer out to me—wore the exact same small silver pendant that had belonged to Ruby, and that was around my throat too: the silver Egyptian ankh.

26. Okay, at that point I was interested in any literature they had to give me.

"Hello," I smiled back.

They both seemed immensely surprised when I accepted the flyer she handed me. I glanced at it.

Twang-Doh—a community of the loving mind.

It didn't take much to engage the women in conversation. They were so happy someone had responded positively to their overture it seemed as though they couldn't believe their luck.

Their accents made it hard to understand them, but I gathered that they wanted to take me to their communal home, as they called it, which, they explained in halting English, was located in Oakland. I didn't think either Percy or Leandros would have advised me to go with them, but I was too excited to refuse.

I was almost positive Ruby had encountered these women—or similar ones—at the airport.

I *tingled* with certainty.

Smiling blandly, I accompanied the gesturing woman to the shuttle to the BART; the other one remained at the airport. My escort didn't say much, but her eyes were sharp and her smile vapid but encouraging. We changed trains once, and I made mental notes of the stops so I could get back to my hotel before nightfall.

I was chatty and curious, even though I didn't understood much of what she said, because of her accent. The leaflet seemed amateurish. But as we rode the trains, she described Twang-Doh as a commune for hardworking seekers of inner peace and prosperity. The leader, Twang, espoused calm, hard work, vegetarianism, meditation, and community. And then she tapped the pendant around my throat, as though we were kindred spirits.

I texted Percy, asking him to do some research for me.

At the West Oakland stop we got out and she led me to a car parked by the curb. Not a car, exactly. More like a white van, with shaded windows. Okay, I started getting a little nervous.

The driver was a super-friendly young Asian man, who jumped out from the front seat when he saw us and enthusiastically slid open the side door of the van, waving me inside.

Was I crazy to get inside?

"I need to make a phone call first," I said, trying to sound normal.

I didn't know if I was more anxious or excited.

The two waited, for me, smiling, while I checked my phone again.

Nothing from Percy yet.

I texted him hastily.

They want me to get in a van to take me to the commune.

28. No response. Where was he? All my previous skeptical thoughts about him flooded through me in a single wave as I tried to decide what to do. Had it all been just too good to be true? Had Percy conned the $5,000 and at this very moment he was laughing it up with Ruby herself?

The anxious mental chatter got intense, and I took a few deep breaths to calm myself. It was almost too warm for my cloak, and I let it flap in the ocean breeze. I was glad I traveled light—I only had my tote with a change of underwear. I wore black stretch jeans, my favorite boots, and a cashmere sweater over a blouse. I didn't own many clothes, but what I had were the best I could get.

As I focused on my breathing, on my clothing, on the soles of my boots firmly planted on the sidewalk, I calmed down. I may have lost my intuitive sense, but I knew that whatever was happening back in New York City, Ruby Wakefield needed me now.

And these two people I'd just met, who still waited patiently, would take me to her.

"Okay," I told them. "I'm ready."

I got in the van, the driver slid the door closed, my guide rode shotgun, and we set off.

I asked them where we were going, and they repeated, very cheerfully, "Twang-Doh."

They tried to talk to me in broken English, but it was too hard to understand.

Still nothing from Percy.

Eventually, we were on a long driveway with manicured shrubs and lots of neat lawn on either side. Up ahead was a large mansion with a huge bronze plaque in front that said "Twang-Doh— Community of God-Mind."

The driver pulled to an abrupt stop, then cheerfully ran around to open the door for me, and bowed me up the steps. There seemed no one else around. My friend from the airport took out a key and unlocked the front door.

We entered, and the first thing I was aware of was the smell of sandalwood and lentils. I hadn't eaten and the lentils smelled good. The sandalwood, not so much.

My escort wanted me to take off my cloak, but my cell phone, passport, and wallet were in the zippered pockets in the lining and I wanted to keep it close by. Nothing about this place felt cozy.

For one thing, I still hadn't seen anyone else. For another, I was hearing the strangest sounds coming from another part of the house.

It was like a soft hum, but it got louder and then

softer. Was it some great machine in the cellar making poisonous candies? What if they made me eat them? My imagination ran wild. The droning sound was so eerie that I wanted to flee.

I was led along a barren hall as the vibrating drone became so loud that I wanted to put my hands to my ears. My guide nodded to a closed door, and put a stubby finger to her lips, as though warning me to be very, *very* quiet.

Then she turned the knob on the door, slowly opened it wide, and ushered me inside.

29. I was at the back of a very large auditorium. Before me was a vast sea of chanting faces, their eyes fluttering, half-closed, their mouths moving in purrs and buzzes and oms.

There must have been at least a hundred people there, of all shapes, sizes, colors, and sounds. The only similarity between all of them was that they wore hand-knitted woolen beanies with their hair tucked inside. I assumed they had hair.

Even if Ruby was one of them, how would I ever recognize her?

I slid into an open area on the floor, knelt, and looked around. My guide found a place close to me, and began chanting as well. The sounds swelled and faded, swelled and faded. I kept my eyes open, wondering where Twang was.

There seemed to be no one person guiding the chanting. It was as though they all knew what to do.

Warily, I took out one of my business cards and wrote the name of the hotel where I was staying on the back. On the front was my name and phone number and a tiny image of a diviner. If I got the chance, I wanted to give it to Ruby, so she could get in touch with me. If I didn't find her, maybe I could give it to someone else who would slip it to her.

The chanting went on for what seemed like hours. Furtively, I checked my phone for messages from Percy, but still nothing had come through.

I felt very much on my own.

After a long time the droning sound began to quiet and eventually I was sitting in a flow of quiet breathing. I heard the inhales and exhales like waves on a beach and then one by one the people stood up and flowed out of the room. No one paid any attention to me, but my guide fused me into the current, which seemed to be following the source of the lentil fragrance I'd noticed earlier.

Ah—a dining hall. I was hungry so I got in the long line with the others, a plastic bowl in my hand. A youngish, chubby woman in front of me smiled sunnily at me as though she wasn't sure whether or not she knew me.

"Hi, I'm new here," I said, wondering if I would meet someone who knew Ruby.

"I'm Snow," she said. "Welcome."

"I'm Tree," the man in front her chimed in.

Snow? Tree? I tried to look serious but wanted to laugh.

"What's your name?" Snow asked.

"City," I said, just for fun.

She looked surprised. "Where are you from?"

"New York. You?"

"Ohio, originally. But I spent a lot of time in Java."

The man in front of me turned around. "I'm Season," he said. "Have you sat with Twang yet? Isn't he amazing?"

I was about to ask if they know Ruby, but if she'd been given a new name, that would make her hard to trace. Maybe that was why the police hadn't been able to find her. I studied each face I came across, wondering if I would recognize the girl from the childhood photo I'd seen. I knew I would recognize the red hair if I saw it, but everyone wore those funny wool beanie hats.

I took my bowl of lentils, and another one of quivering red jello, to one of the long tables. My guide sat across from me, smiling silently. My neighbors were a middle-aged man from Canada on my right and another young woman on my left. The girl's eyes were shiny and gray, and it was hard to tell whether she wanted to cry or they were glistening with joy. I figured she was closer in age to Ruby so I focused my attention on her.

"What's it like here? How do you spend most of your day, besides chanting?"

She was enthusiastic. "We have chores, and we have lots of time to meditate. At least once a day we get to be with Twang. That's the best part of the day."

"Are you from around here? How did you find out about Twang?"

"Yeah, I'm local. My parents threw me out. They didn't like what I was doing with my life."

"What were you doing?"

"Crack cocaine and lots of sex."

"And Twang rescued you?"

"Grace did—she's one of his assistants. I was at a homeless shelter. She brought me here. They've all been so great to me. I never want to leave. The only thing I promised is never to do drugs again."

"Is there a religion to this place?" I asked.

The Canadian on the other side answered. "Absolutely not. There is no dogma here. All that's asked is you trust in our mind-soul creator and in yourself. And each other—it's a wonderful community."

"Yes, I heard it was cool. A friend's daughter joined. But you don't know each other's real names, right? So if I asked you, you wouldn't know it?"

"Our real names are the ones we're given when we put on our hats," the girl said gravely. "We're not allowed to use the old ones."

"Ruby," I said anyway, on the off-chance. "And her mom had red hair."

"Wheat has red hair," said the Canadian. "She's wearing a red hat. Sweet kid."

Wheat.

Well. I should have guessed that myself.

"Can you introduce me to her?"

But people were dispersing to do their chores and

the Canadian shook his head. "We're all kept pretty busy for the next few hours. I have to go myself. Yard work."

I got up too and asked my guide for a tour. She kept close to my side, answering my questions as best she could as she showed me through the kitchen, a common area, the dormitory-style rooms upstairs, and the vegetable gardens.

As I pretended to be super-interested in the greenhouses, I sought out everyone with a red hat, hoping to recognize Ruby's wide-eyed gaze. In one hand I clutched the business card on which I written the name of my hotel. It was so unlikely I'd be able to give it to her, but I wanted to have it ready, just in case.

I was about to ask whether I could meet Twang, when I spotted a slim figure with a red hat in the doorway to the main meditation room. She was regarding me curiously.

I swung over toward her.

"Ruby!" I hissed.

She leapt back, startled, so I *knew* it was her. I strode toward her, where she stood frozen, and slipped my business card and the ankh chain into her palm, hoping no one saw me.

Right on my heels, my guide grabbed my arm. She clucked and clucked, shocked and upset. In broken English, she told me it was against the rules to use anyone's Christian name in the house.

Someone else appeared, seemingly out of nowhere, and whisked Ruby away. My guide ushered me out the front door, which she slammed in my face.

Well.

I had found her.

29. I paused in front of the mansion and looked around, wondering how on earth I was going to get back to my airport hotel. The sun was heading westward, and I didn't like the fact that I had no idea where I was.

I checked my phone. Still no word from Percy.

And no sign of the white van that had brought me here.

I set off down the cement driveway, and focused on my boots and my breathing instead of on the sensation of being lost. It was at these kinds of moments I longed to be able to trust my inner guide again. All my life it had been there for me. Not a computerized voice impersonating a British female, but more like a sensation, or a smell or instinct.

But I experienced nothing.

Instead, I walked down the driveway toward the road, and when I got to the street I looked up and down the rows of elegant houses. The sidewalk shimmered from a fresh rain that must have splashed down when I was still inside the house.

Now what?

I heard the sound of a car, and a moment later the white van popped into view. The same driver who had brought me here pulled over and rolled down his window.

"Need ride?" he asked in his hard-to-understand accent.

"Yes, please, to the subway would be great," I replied gratefully.

He did better than that, though, he took me all the way across the Bay Bridge and back into the city. He talked the entire time, in an earnest, friendly way. I think he was telling me how wonderful Twang was, and why I needed to go back to talk to him. Even just to meet him, to sit in his presence. Yes, if I did that, my life would be changed forever.

Things like that.

I tuned him out, wishing Percy would call. I asked the driver to drop me off near the wharf, where I knew there was a BART station. I was vaguely anxious that the driver might be planning to kidnap me and drag me back to the commune, but he came around to open the door for me, shook my gloved hand, and took off with a wave.

A huge feeling of relief filled me when he'd gone. I turned toward the bay, wondering what to do now.

I walked a little way, and the city lights began to twinkle on the hills. The Golden Gate Bridge loomed to my left and the city was at my back. A chill started to set in, and I was glad of my cloak. I felt peaceful, almost floating.

I sat on a stone bench and took out my phone.

Still no word from Percy.

What was my gut telling me?

I listened hard but all I sensed was that I was hungry again, in spite of the earlier lentils and jello. Trusting my phone app that scouted for good vegetarian restaurants, I got up and headed toward the nearest one. It smelled delicious and I ordered quinoa and okra in a curry sauce.

While I waited, sipping jasmine tea, I read through Percy's texts again.

Where was he, anyway? Why hadn't he called me back or at least texted?

Feeling hopelessly deceived, I called him for the twentieth time.

And this time he answered.

"Where have you been?" I demanded.

"Getting the cast on." He sounded groggy.

"Oh. Right."

"Took longer than I thought, and then I was in recovery for a while. When I got back here I fell asleep. Just woke up. What's up?"

I was so glad to hear his voice and to know that he was back at my house and everything was normal again, that my frustration faded rapidly.

"I found her."

"Good. I knew you would. Where is she?"

I described what had happened since I arrived.

"So you weren't able to talk to her?" he asked.

"No. Twang-Doh is definitely a cult, and Twang's a masterful leader. She's been brainwashed, but they all look healthy—no one's being drugged or beaten, as far as I could see."

"Are you going to tell the police you found her?"

"Yes, but not yet. I want to try to talk to her first. I'm afraid once the police get hold of her I may not have access to her again."

"Does she know her father is dead?"

"I don't know. My guess is that Twang-Doh keeps news and social media well-hidden. I didn't see a single screen."

My dish arrived but I didn't hang up. I wished Percy were with me and we could talk this over together in person.

"How's the ankle feeling?" I asked, my mouth full.

"Better, thanks. The drugs help." He was silent a moment and then asked, "So what are you going to do now?"

"That's what I was going to ask you. I wondered, is there a connection between Wolcott Candies and Twang? Is there any way to link him to my PayPal account? How does that work?"

"I don't think so, but I'll try to find out."

I was already feeling a lot more cheerful with the taste of curry and the heft of the quinoa in my belly.

"I think I need to actually talk with Ruby," I said. "I want to be the one to tell her about her father, and maybe I can do it more gently than the cops can. I also want to be sure she's where she wants to be. Joining a cult is not a bad thing if you're escaping from a lousy family situation. She just might be safer where she is. But I want to be sure."

"She's a senior in college. That means she's not escaping from a lousy family situation."

"Not anymore, maybe. But maybe she went there

a while back, and now it's a place where she feels safe."

"Safe from what?"

"Or from who?" I was thinking of the man who had mugged me.

"Her mother lives in San Francisco. Are you going to tell her you know where her daughter is?"

"Ruby may be more scared of her mother than her father."

"You think she's scared?"

"She'd have to be, to disappear like that."

"Maybe she's just a rebel. Or a druggie."

"She's not a drug addict," I told him. "I can tell." I finished the last of the quinoa and pushed the plate away. "Think I should go see her mother? She *has* to care, doesn't she?"

"Okay."

"I mean, if your daughter's missing, wouldn't you be frantic?"

"Maybe. I wouldn't know."

"Well, I think I need to find out."

"Okay," he said again. "Coming back tomorrow? I can change your flight if you want to stay longer."

"Thank you—I'll let you know. I'm not coming back until I've spoken with Ruby, though."

30. When I went back outside night had fallen and it was raining again. I heard the foghorns in the distance, the wailing sound filling my breast with yearning. Foghorns did that to me—as though calling me to adventure and warning me not to go, at the same time.

I debated calling the number Percy texted me for Ruby's mother, Vivian Blum, but I figured she might refuse to see me if I did that, and so instead I splurged on a taxi to the address he'd provided. Now that I felt I had officially earned that $5,000 Joel agreed to pay me for finding his daughter, I didn't mind spending it.

The porch light was on and there was a Christmas wreath still hanging on the front door.

I asked the driver to wait, and rang the bell. A plump face peered at me through glass panes of the outer door. She looked puzzled and suspicious. Of course in my dark cloak I probably did look a little odd. I let the velvet hood fall back so she could see my head more clearly in the light.

Cautiously she opened the door. "Yes?"

"Hello, Ms. Blum. My name is Satyana. I wanted to tell you that I know where your daughter is."

She flinched as though I struck her. "Yes?" she said again.

"May I come in?" I asked politely.

She opened the door slightly, so we were standing in the small entryway. She obviously didn't want me to come any further.

Right away I could tell from her crossed arms and feigned surprise that she already knew where Ruby was. She was dumpy—not fat but formless, with eyes that were squashed between heavy lids and fleshy circles under the eyes. Her sweat pants and pale blue sweatshirt did not look as though they were worn for exercise.

"I'm sorry to bother you," I said. "Your ex-husband asked me to find her, and then he died before I could finish the job for him. I thought I would let you know instead." I scanned her curiously. "Seems to me he could have just asked you, if you already knew. Why didn't he?"

She teared up, and her face became reddish. For some reason my words sparked emotion in her.

"Where is she?" she demanded. It seemed more of a challenge to see if I really knew than because she was interested.

"She's at the Twang-Doh house. But you knew that, of course. Does it bother you?"

"Why would it bother me?"

"That your daughter's joined a cult?" I ventured.

"She's being fed, dressed, made to work, given good food, and a bed to sleep in. That's all she needs right now." She screwed her puffy eyes into slits, half angry, half worried. "They take good care of her."

"Really?" I asked.

"Twang is a good man. A very good man, no

matter what people say."

"Okay…"

"Are you going to tell the police you've found her? I know they're looking for her."

"Would you rather she was left there?"

"She's not a child. And she deserves privacy."

"Does she know about her father?"

"I'll tell her, in time. What's the rush? Her knowing isn't going to bring him back."

True enough. Still, when a family member dies, the usual thing is to let the other family members know. There was something more to this woman's reluctance than indifference, either to her ex-husband or to her daughter.

She was protecting her daughter from something. But what?

I knew she wasn't going to tell me.

"I won't bother you anymore," I said, realizing she was inching the door closed in my face. "Good night."

The cab was still on the street, the driver reading a newspaper in the dim overhead light. I was glad I asked him to wait, since this area seemed traffic-free. I got in and gave him the name of my hotel. I was thinking about Ruby and how strange it must be to grow up with parents like hers, who didn't seem to have the first clue about parenting. But then, who does?

Learning back and closing my eyes, I longed to talk with someone about the encounter.

My phone buzzed and I opened my eyes. *Unknown number.*

I answered.

"Hello?"

A breathless young girl's voice said, "Ms. Satyana?"

"This is Satyana."

"May I come and see you? I'm near your hotel. Are you there?"

"Who is this?"

"Ruby Wakefield."

31.

I glanced out the fogged-up window and recognized nothing. The driver had opted to take the freeway. "How far are we from the hotel?" I asked him.

"Five minutes."

I spoke into the phone. "I'm almost there, Ruby. Room 304."

When I was dropped off, I looked around the rainy driveway but didn't see any sign of Ruby. She wasn't in the lobby either. I took the elevator to my floor, and there she was, sitting cross-legged on the carpet across from my door, her back against the wall, her eyes closed.

"Hello," I said gently.

She turned to look at me and stared without moving for a long moment. Then, slowly, she uncoiled her legs and stood up, still gazing at me with wide blue eyes. She had removed the red beanie, and her hair fell in luxuriant auburn waves well past her shoulders. She had a small, squarish face and wore a big baggy wool sweater that was wet from rain.

I wondered why she stared—whether she was high on something—but then she said my name under her breath, as though mesmerized.

"Satyana."

I couldn't help myself: I hugged her. I *had* to—she seemed so slight and forlorn. And what I had to tell her was so damned sad.

"They don't like it when I leave the house," she said, as I slid the card key into my lock and we went inside the room. "This time it was extra hard. But I wanted to see you."

I took off my cloak and draped it over the back of the desk chair, then we each sat on one of the wide beds, our knees almost touching. "Why?"

"I want to know about my father. Did he send you?"

"I have some sad news for you."

"What?" Her big eyes widened, but in them there was no light, and I was pretty sure she already knew.

"He's dead, Ruby. I'm so sorry."

"I had to make sure." She looked as though she was going to cry.

"So you did know. How did you find out?"

"There's an Internet café I go to when I can. That's how I stay in touch with my mom. They don't like me connecting with the outer world. But sometimes I just have to." She sounded defensive, as though I might criticize her for leaving the protection of the commune.

"I saw him the day before he died," I said gently. "He was worried about you and wanted me to try to find you."

Her eyes filled again and she blinked hard. "I didn't think he cared."

"Oh, he cared all right," I assured her, in spite of my own doubts. "Tell me how you ended up at Twang-Doh? Have you been there for a while?"

"I was there a few years ago. My mom had a boyfriend who... well, anyway, I ran away. They took me in—they were so great. But my dad found me and made me move in with him instead. Then I went to college and everything changed anyway."

"Why are you there now?"

She looked at me as though she was surprised I didn't know. "I had a fight with my dad. Told him I wanted to drop out of college. He was really mad 'cos I only have a few more months left before I get my degree. He yelled ... I hated that. He said he wasn't going to give me any more money. I got on a bus and went back to Twang."

It all made so much sense. And yet...

"Your dad must have known that's where you'd go," I said.

"I don't know. Maybe. I've been giving them money, about fifty dollars a month, to support some good programs they have. Like helping runaway teens. When I told them I needed to be there again, they took me in right away. They take really good care of me there."

"But what about your college—aren't you taken care of there, too?"

"No, it's not the same." She looked as though she was going to cry again. "Why did he die? Why would anyone want to kill him? I don't understand."

"I don't understand either. That's another reason I wanted to find you. I thought maybe you could help me figure out who killed him and why."

She couldn't restrain her tears. I brought her a box of tissues from the bathroom and sat beside her, letting her sob. I sensed her grief, and rage filled me—at her father, her mother, but most of all at Twang.

I used my soothing Voice, murmuring reassurances and positive encouragement for a long time.

When she was quieter I put my arms around her. She leaned her head on my shoulder and her breathing began to get calmer too.

"So you think your father really didn't know you were at the commune? Your mother didn't tell him?"

"I don't think so. She kind of likes me being there. It's safe."

"Why do you think he wanted me to try to find you?"

"Probably 'cos he really didn't like me dropping out of school. I only had one semester left of college and he'd already paid for the whole year. He probably didn't want to waste the tuition money." She looked at me through her tears. "He probably thought you could talk me into going back."

"Anyway, why do you want to drop out? Why not take a leave of absence for a few months? Go back next fall."

"Twang doesn't believe in college. When I first met him, I told him I had one year left and he said that was okay. But now that I'm falling apart he doesn't think it's good for me. Too much stress."

"What's your degree?"

"Architecture. I was into sustainable building. I want to redesign Twang's place eventually, so that it's completely self-sustaining." She blew her nose again, and stood up. "I really need to get back. They don't like it when I'm late."

"What do they do?"

"Usually it's work punishment," she said. "Sometimes I'm required to stay in my room."

"But you can leave any time?"

She nodded. Her hard, wet eyes softened and she sighed, helplessly. "They're like my family, the one I never really had. They're strict, but they take care of me. They make me believe in myself. I know people think it's a cult, and maybe it is, because I really do believe in what they believe in. Hard work, prayer, and community living. And if you sit in Twang's presence, even for a few minutes, you start feeling so good."

I wondered what they gave her to drink just before she sat in Twang's presence.

She put on her pea coat and tucked her gorgeous locks into the wool hat. "So in a way I can't leave," she confessed. "I don't know where I'd go or what I'd do without Twang. I don't even mind the sex anymore."

Her voice was low key, with no inflection, but her words shocked me.

"He has sex with you?"

"With everyone. It's another way to get close to God. He doesn't claim to be God, he knows he's a man. But he's able to show us how we can get closer to God. I'm learning, day by day."

I leapt past her and barred her way out. "You don't have to go back," I said urgently.

My urgency made her anxious. "You don't understand, I *want* to go back. It's my home now."

"You have a future in front of you. You're pretty, you're young."

"Not really."

I put my hand on her arm. "Ruby, something happened to you. I can see that—something terrible. When you were young … I may be way off-base here, but that's what I'm seeing. But that's over now. You're not a child any more. Now you can take control of what's happening."

Her eyes widened in shock and she began trembling. "How—*no one* knows…" she whispered.

"It's true, isn't it? And I want to help you. I promised your father I would. He wasn't asking me to find you, of course he knew where you were. But he wanted me to get you out of there. And I can."

"But way back then he sent me back to Mom's…" her voice was barely audible, "…and her boyfriend…"

"That's over now. You're not a child any longer. You don't have to go back. Not to your mom's—and not to Twang. You're *free* now."

She shook her head and pushed past me to open the door. "No, I'm really not."

"Ruby, wait. People always prefer what they know, even if it's unpleasant, to what's unknown. But I can help you."

"I don't think so." She was in the hall now, backing toward the elevator.

I longed to restrain her, call her mother, call the police. Anything to stop her from returning. But I knew that would only drive her deeper into the monster's belly. He made me sick.

I took a deep breath and tried to calm myself. I wouldn't be able to help her if I succumbed to rage. I knew that. I had to remain detached. Angry, yes, but calm.

"Call me any time," I called after her. "Keep my phone number with you. And remember this, dear: *You are always free in your thoughts.*"

32.

She gave me a startled look, so I knew my words had reached her even if they didn't have an immediate impact. I watched her walk hurriedly along the beige hall to the elevator bank. Going back inside my room and closing the door, I wondered how she would return to the house, whether she would be punished, or whether she would be quietly greeted by the stony impassive strangers whose familiarity made her feel at home.

I was tempted to call her mother and tell her that her daughter was being raped by the cult leader whom she so admired, but I decided not to. For two reasons: One, she wouldn't believe me. Two, if she did believe me, I had the feeling she would probably blame her daughter.

And if either she or I called the police to arrest Twang, they would find no evidence, I was sure of that.

Ruby herself would deny what she told me.

I called Percy even though it was almost midnight on the east coast. He sounded wide-awake, as though he'd been waiting for my call.

"Any luck?"

"I saw her mother. She obviously knew where Ruby was before I told her and doesn't mind. I think she's just glad to have her out of her hair. She said she didn't think it was important for Ruby to know her father was dead."

"And?"

"When I got back to the hotel, guess who was waiting for me? Ruby."

"You're kidding."

"Nope. There she was, sitting outside my hotel room. We chatted for a while. She already knew about her father. I guessed as much."

"How did she find out?"

"She says on the Internet—at a café she goes to. It was on the news so that doesn't surprise me. Isn't that the saddest thing ever?"

"I'm glad you were there for her, even if just for a short time," Percy said impulsively. "You have a way of making people feel that everything's going to be okay."

"What about you?" I asked. "Have you found out anything more?"

"Yep—we know Joel Wakefield had a ton of investments. You know, the old-fashioned pork belly kind."

"He owns pork bellies?"

"No, but he invested in artificial sweetener. The kind that's used to make candy."

I wrinkled my nose. "Interesting…"

"He was in over his head in the sweetener department. He also owned half the stock of Wolcott."

"Oh."

"I know."

"Who inherits his investments?" I asked.

"His daughter."

"So if money is the motive, she's the main suspect. But I know she's innocent."

"Sure about that?"

"Yes."

"You're the intuitive. By the way, that detective called again. He's really pissed you left town. He's setting the wheels in motion to freeze your account."

"Can he do that?"

"He's trying. I tried to point out that the money is yours and he has no right, but he's making the threat."

I sighed deeply. I hated calling in favors from friends, and especially from Leandros, but he was the one person I knew who would be able to get the detective off my back.

"I'll ask Leandros what to do," I told Percy. "And I'm coming back tomorrow morning. There's no point in staying here any longer, now that I've met with Ruby."

"I guess not. You're not going to try to see Twang?"

"What good would that do?"

"Yeah, come back home. If you don't want people to know where the girl is, you'd better not blaze a trail to her."

"I don't know why I'm so protective of her. But she doesn't have anyone else. Her mother had an awful boyfriend, and then kicked Ruby out when she was still a kid. Her father didn't understand her. She went to college much too young. No wonder she's looking for family."

"Are you going to tell the detective you found her?"

"Maybe, but not where she is. I'm afraid they might pin the murder on her, especially if she stands to inherit a pile of money from investments in Wolcott. And she didn't do it, Percy. I know she didn't kill her father."

I was still too keyed-up to sleep so I called Leandros next. It turned out he was in Palm Springs at a convention but also on vacation. He played as hard as he worked.

I told him that Detective Cleveland was

threatening to freeze my meager account and that he believed I was a con. I started explaining why I wasn't, but he cut me off with a laugh.

"Don't worry, Sati. I'll take care of it."

"Really?"

"Text me his name and the precinct he works out of. I have to be in New York later this week anyway, so I'll arrange to see him. Maybe we can chat with him together. Have coffee or something."

Leandros could make even a threatening police detective seem sweet as a kitten. I doubted he had an appointment—he was just saying that so I didn't think he was coming just to see me. I smiled into the phone.

"That would be great."

"So I found out a couple of things for you. For one, Wolcott Candies is going under. They're about to declare bankruptcy."

"Whoa. What does that mean?"

"I'm not sure yet. I also found out that your murder victim went to Hawai'i to see his half-brother, John Henry, a few weeks ago. And they had a fight."

"About what?"

"They were in his office and a receptionist overheard them. She doesn't know what it was about. The insurance company he works for is solid."

"Okay. Well, thanks."

"I'll call you when I land in New York. We'll have lunch."

Even though Leandros is my best friend, I still can't get used to how much money he has and how easy it is for him to hop on a plane and go somewhere. He has no idea what it's like to be worried about paying a bill on time.

That's not true—he grew up like that, and he doesn't want to go back to it. He loves living the life he has. I don't blame him.

I just sometimes wish it were mine, too.

33.

To my amazed delight, Percy had scrounged up three clients for the rest of the week, one each day. I never thought he'd be able to do it. Not only that, but these were people I didn't already know.

"How did you find them?" I asked in amazement.

"Oh, the usual," he said modestly.

Things were looking up. Three clients in one week!

My first one was a young woman, about Percy's age, with long dark hair, pretty blue eyes, and a dilemma about whether to stay in New York City at a job she didn't care for, or move back to Ohio, where she was from, and get a degree in social work. The downside of returning was that she'd have to live with her parents, with whom she did not get along. But it would only be for a year. What did I advise her to do?

I laid out the cards on the oak chest, grew quiet, and tried to let the light inside me glimmer. Nothing. Still, as I gazed at the cards, not really seeing them, I asked her some questions, seemingly irrelevant things, like about the weather in Ohio, where she'd just spent the holidays, whether she had a boyfriend. After a while, she started talking without me asking anything.

"I want to go back," she said at last. "I realize from talking to you that I need to leave New York. But I'm dreading falling back into old patterns. My parents are so overbearing…"

She trailed off and I waited, then pointed to the five of wands. She looked at it.

"What does it mean?" she asked.

"Look at it. You'll know." There was a long silence. "Think outside the box. There are many ways of doing one thing. What are some options for you?"

"That I could go back, but I don't have to live with my parents? But they'd be so upset."

"Probably."

She sighed. "I thought about that, but it would be really hard. You don't know what they're like. Also, financially it would be so much harder to go to school."

We talked for a while longer, as a clarity and courage grew inside her. Eventually, she realized that she could be independent from her family even in her hometown.

At a few minutes before her hour was up, I heard the singing bowl from the outer office. Percy was signaling that her time was up.

She left feeling grateful and encouraged, and through the open door, I heard Percy suggest a follow-up appointment in two weeks. I smiled to myself. I could tell from the way they talked that they knew each other. But they didn't sound too familiar, so they couldn't have known each other for long.

When she had left I went into reception area. "How do you know her?" I asked.

He looked up and his cheeks were pink. Maybe he just had a little crush. I felt a weird ping of jealousy, which was ridiculous. I didn't want to think about Percy in that way.

"I did a little promotion on Facebook and she opted in," he said.

"What sort of promotion?"

"A client can come and see you three times in a month for just $150. I know that's a huge rate drop for you, but a smart promotion, at least till the end of this month. I'm hoping people will give it to their friends as a gift."

$150 was a lot more than zero. Percy got up from behind the desk and handed me two checks.

"What's that for?"

"From the client you just saw."

"And the other one?"

"My rent check." He looked surprised. "I'm not going to stay in your apartment for free."

"But that's temporary, until your leg's better," I said. "You're already paying rent on another apartment."

"That one's cheap. I can afford this. I'd feel weird

if I didn't pay, so take it."

"But what about our business agreement? You're working for me now—what if you don't get enough clients and I can't pay you?"

Percy crushed the check into my palm with a short laugh. "I'll get you plenty of clients."

"How can you be so sure?"

"You have great potential here that you haven't tapped into. I feel I'm in a mysterious cave where I know there's gold, and all I have to do is knock and it will reveal itself." He sounded a little like I did when I gave a reading and I was suspicious. But he looked at me so innocently that I backed down.

His confidence inspired me.

So did my growing bank account.

Yes, things were definitely looking up.

34.

Despite our rocky history, I love it when Leandros comes to town. For one thing, he takes me to restaurants I could never afford. Like the chic Ethiopian place where we weren't given utensils and instead ate with our fingers out of the same bowl, which was oddly sexy, and ridiculously expensive. Or one of my favorites: dancing in the summer twilight while cruising around the island of Manhattan. Even when I was married, we'd meet on occasion—just as friends. Always, now, just friends.

A few inches of snow had fallen overnight, making the sidewalks appear freshly cleaned. The sky was a bright blue and the cold not as intense as it had been the past few days.

He said he was there for an engagement at his branch office, to which I had never been, and we met for drinks at Ma Maison, a French bistro around the corner.

When he saw me, he teased me about my cloak, as he usually did.

"No broomstick today?" He grinned and kissed my cheek. "Don't tell me you had to use the subway?"

I smiled serenely, returned his hug, and allowed him to remove the cloak and hang it on the coat rack by the front door. It was piled high with other peoples' slippery down and wet wool.

He had already enjoyed half a Talisker single malt. I ordered champagne, as usual.

"So I found out more about your friend, Mr. Henry," he began, tucking his knee between my velvet leggings in his typically intimate, but casual way. Sometimes I wondered what his wife would think if she saw us together, because Leandros could be such a flirt. And yet he had always been loyal to her—as far as I knew, anyway.

"And?"

"One thing my man reported is he seems scared. Like a jumpy rabbit, pink nose, all twitchy, and trembling fur."

"He has fur?"

"On his head—it's a piece. It looks like fur. White."

"I don't believe it. How can he be sure it's a rug?" I'm already giddy just being with him, and I've barely had any champagne.

"Trust me." He grinned too, his eyes the color of hot gray steam.

I sometimes thought his grin was why he was so successful at being a lawyer. He'd turn that smile on a suspect and they'd admit to anything.

"So, what did he say?" I focused on my glass. "Did you ask him about that fight with Joel?"

"The secretary who overheard thought it might have something to do with the daughter. What's she like?"

"Seems like a nice, intelligent girl. Pretty too, round face, with big blue eyes." He grinned at me again, warming me all over. I knew what he was thinking: she was the opposite of me, with my thin face, strong nose, and narrow eyes.

"I got us tickets to a Broadway show," he said. "Are you hungry or should we eat afterward?"

I loved late night dinners so I told him we could wait. He discreetly slipped a couple of hundreds into the leather check holder, and tenderly wrapped the cloak around my shoulders as though I were a queen. We set off down Fifth Avenue, our arms linked.

"I don't really know where to go from here," I said as we walked. "As far as I know, the police have no leads at all as to who killed Joel Wakefield. How can that be? There were plenty of people in the diner where he was shot."

"We mentioned the possibility of an execution last time we talked. What do you think now?"

"Percy has investigated inside and out and hasn't discovered a single hint of organized crime. I'm sure he would have by now, if there were one."

I felt Leandros's arm tighten slightly. "Who's Percy?"

"He's my new personal assistant," I replied nonchalantly.

"Since when?"

"Last week. He's smart, very attractive, and I even think he likes me."

Leandros didn't bite. "Where did you find him?"

I briefly recounted how Percy fell off my stoop. "He's on disability from UPS and is working for me until his ankle is fixed and he can get back to his job. He moved into my garden apartment."

"Sounds very fast."

It *had* all happened very quickly, I had to agree. "And he's been great helping me try to find Joel Wakefield's daughter. He's quite the detective himself."

Leandros grunted but didn't probe further. At the theater I let him take charge of the tickets, and we paused for another glass of champagne in the lounge, then took the drinks into the theater.

Our seats were the best in the house: a private box in the gallery, close to the stage, where you could see everything, you didn't get spat on, and you watched as though you were in a dream.

35.

Afterward, over pulpo a la gallega (him) and espinacas con garbanzos (me) and a bottle of Gran Reserva Gran Codorníu (both of us), we had fun tearing the play to bits and pieces and stepping on them.

We were at a darling Spanish restaurant on 8th Avenue. Leandros loved taking me to these kinds of places. It wasn't that he was showing off—he knew how much I enjoyed them.

When our cattiness about the play petered out, we turned back to the situation at hand, which was much more interesting to both of us.

"So I'm having breakfast with Detective Cleveland tomorrow," he said. "You'll join us, right?

"Where?"

"At my hotel. I'm staying at the Paramount. I invited him there."

"Does he know I'm coming too?"

"Who cares? I don't like his insinuation that you're trying to embezzle a murdered man's money."

"I don't like it either."

"Don't worry." Leandros smiled tenderly. "I'll protect you."

I focused on my glass, flushing. "Thanks." Somehow he always made me feel like a young girl.

"You don't think Ruby had a hand in extracting

the money?" he asked.

"Leandros, we're talking about a paltry $5,000 here. No one cares except Detective Cleveland."

"And the guy who accosted you with the gun!"

"That's true. Yes."

"What I really want to know is who killed him."

"Yes, and why."

"Maybe Cleveland will have more insights for us tomorrow."

By the time we had lingered over coffee and peras al vino dulce, it was way after midnight. Still, neither of us really wanted to part. We rarely got to spend this much time together, and it was like being on a vacation.

"Want to check out some jazz?" he asked.

I did, and so we headed south toward Greenwich Village. Somehow, even though I lived there, Leandros was the one who always knew the right place to hang out at on a Friday night. The cab dropped us off in front of a club he had found on his cell phone, and the sinuous caressing sounds of a saxophone drifted out to meet us. The club was small, crowded, dark, and we stood for a while, sipping more sparkles, and leaning into each other, but not too much, until a table was free.

And that was when I saw him.

"Leandros," I whispered. "The guy who threatened me with a gun last week—he's at the door. He's watching me."

36. Leandros glanced at the door, then back at me. "Are you sure?"

I felt dizzy, and this time it was not from Leandros's friendly compliments. "I'm sure. He doesn't have a beard this time, but I can tell. I'm scared."

"Don't worry, I won't let him hurt you. I'm going to call 911." He got out his phone.

"Forget it, he's gone," I said. I was shaking.

"Come on, let's get out of here. I'll take you home."

"But how did he know I was here?"

"He could have traced you via your phone. Or it could be a coincidence."

"It's not a coincidence."

"Come on."

"I don't want to go yet. What if he's waiting outside?"

"I'll call for an officer to escort us."

I don't know how Leandros manages this kind of thing. Within half an hour, a police officer had arrived at the club and escorted us outside, to the surprised looks of the other patrons. A police car waited by the curb, and Leandros and I piled in the back seat. The officer got in front, next to the driver. My house was not far from the club, but we drove slowly, all of us scouring the sidewalks.

"Describe the man who attacked you," the driver asked.

"Short, wearing a down coat, I think it was dark blue. He had a beard last time, but not this time. I recognized him right away, though. He looked so angry—he was definitely looking for me."

"But you say you don't know him?"

"No, I've only seen him once before. The police have that report. It happened a week ago."

The police car turned onto Gay Street, which was deserted as usual. We stopped in front of my house.

"We'll wait till you're safely inside, ma'am," the officer assured me.

"Thank you very much."

We got out and I quickly ran up the stairs, key in hand. I longed to get safely inside. Leandros stood close while I unlocked and opened the door.

He reached around me and turned on the hall light.

"Feels okay in there?" he asked, concerned.

I stepped inside. "No one's here." I could feel it. "And Percy's downstairs."

"Good. I'll take a quick look around anyway."

Briefly, he turned on the light in the office, and then went up the stairs, two at a time. I waited by the front door. He came down a few minutes later.

"All clear. You're okay."

"Thanks, Leandros. When are we meeting Mr. Detective?"

"Eight, at my hotel." He gave me a brief hug, smiled warmly into my eyes, and backed out the door. "Don't forget to lock up, okay?"

I nodded, closed and locked the door from the inside, and threw both bolts.

The light had been out in Percy's apartment, so I figured he was already asleep. Still, it felt good knowing he was nearby. I went over to the window in the front room to draw the curtains and looked out at the snowy street. Leandros was heading toward Christopher Street and the squad car rolled slowly toward Waverly.

It had begun to snow again, a light dusting that flickered in the street lamp and made everything seem so pretty it was like being in an illustration.

Leandros disappeared around the corner and the street was empty again.

37.

Even though he hadn't seen me for a week, Detective Cleveland still did not like me. His dark eyes under heavy slabs of eyebrows were sharp as nails and just as unpleasant. He'd shaved though, which showed his dark chin to advantage, and he'd put on a flannel sports jacket.

But even spruced up for breakfast with a celebrity lawyer, it was still obvious that he thought I somehow had managed to fraudulently nab $5,000 from a dead man's account, and he was not going to let that slip past him.

It took two cups of delicious wood-roasted espresso and Leandros's good-natured but very firm voice to soften him even slightly. When he described the man I'd seen in the club last night, Cleveland began to act more civilly toward me.

"When did you see him before last night?"

"A week ago. I was mugged near First Avenue. I reported it to the police."

"And you're sure it was the same man?"

"Yes."

"Coincidence, maybe."

"I don't think so. He didn't want my purse or credit card—he asked for $5,000. He acted as though it belonged to him."

Cleveland's black eyes were still nail-hard, but his voice changed. "How did he know about the $5,000?"

"That's what I want to know, too," I said.

"Why didn't you report this earlier?" Cleveland demanded.

"It was too weird," I replied, instead of telling him I didn't think he'd believe me.

"If we could figure out who transferred the money into Sati's PayPal, we'd have something to go on," Leandros suggested.

"It looked as though the victim did it himself," Cleveland said. "But how could he? He was dead at the time."

We turned to the carmelized onion focaccia, and sipped our espressos, and then I said: "I found Joel Wakefield's daughter."

Cleveland looked skeptical. "She's alive?"

"Yes. She's okay. I'd rather not tell you where she is, though. Do I have to?"

He frowned. "Why not?"

"I'm being protective. She's okay where she is—at least for now. And to be removed from there, which is what you'd do, I think, probably isn't the best thing for her." I added: "At least for now." I still had a vague hope that I'd somehow be able to get her to return for her last semester at Williams College. I even had an odd image of attending her graduation ceremony...

I shook myself and came back to my omelet.

Cleveland harrumphed but his expression wasn't as hostile. "Can you tell me in confidence? I don't have to share it except to make sure I'm satisfied, and then end our search. That's fair, isn't it?"

I looked at Leandros, who gave a barely perceptible nod. It seemed he felt we could trust the detective. I told him about the commune and Ruby's strange comfort in being there.

"I can't promise not to check on her," he said, grimly, when I was finished. "But believe it or not, I'll try to do it discreetly. How did you find her?"

I was about to describe the thread of events that led me to her, but Leandros answered for me: "She's intuitive, you know."

Cleveland harrumphed again and said, "Anyway, I'm more interested in the guy you saw last night. The one who attacked you last week. He's the one who can really tell us what happened."

"What do you mean?"

Cleveland took out his phone, and scrolled for a photo. He passed it to Leandros, who passed it to me.

"That the guy?"

I studied the police drawing, then nodded, feeling sick. "Yes, that's him."

"He murdered Joel Wakefield."

I felt even sicker.

"Are you sure?" Leandros asked.

"Pretty sure—from reports of witnesses. If you run into him again, will you call me?" He handed me a card.

I nodded again. "I really hope I don't, though."

Cleveland smiled tightly, shook both our hands, and took off. We left soon after. It was a bright sunny morning, and the chill didn't feel all that bad. Leandros tucked my gloved hand in his, and patted it.

"Let's go to your place," he suggested. "I want to meet your new assistant."

38.

But when we got to my house, Percy was not in the office. I was disappointed because I wanted Leandros to see how businesslike my new set-up was, with an actual receptionist. But even without Percy there, Leandros was impressed. I could tell by the way he paused to admire the clean lines of the desk by the window, its top cleared of all clutter. Percy had moved the ottoman back between the two scissor chairs and put my New Yorkers in a fan on top of it. It looked like a real, legitimate waiting room.

"Ward Bennett?" Leandros asked, examining at the chairs and desk. When I nodded, he said, "Love it all. Perfect for you. I half noticed last night, but now I can really see it, it's just great."

He went inside the redesigned office and looked around. His painting of the lighthouse still hung over the mantel and he went over to it.

"That old thing," he said, scrunching his eyes and surveying it critically.

"Looks good, doesn't it?"

"It's okay."

Upstairs he sat at the kitchen table and I made coffee—he was an addict. I texted Percy, inviting him to join us. He texted back that he was out with some friends and would be back later.

"My plane leaves at four," Leandros said, glancing at the elaborately complex Girard-Perregaux on his tanned wrist. "How about a quick game of chess?"

Chess was one of our favorite games, and we always tried to play when we're together. I got out the pieces. They were a gift from him, many years ago, on my twenty-first birthday. That was before we'd split and he'd opted for marriage with a wealthy beautiful socialite he'd met in Los Angeles. The set was made of marble, the Romans in a dark ocean green and the Anglo-Saxons in pale ivory yellow.

We hadn't played in a few months, so I turned all my attention to the game. The logic I summoned helped to ground me, and cleared my thinking.

I started. I moved a pawn one space forward. He responded by leaping his queen's pawn two spaces toward mine. I challenged his pawn with my knight.

"What's your impression of Detective Cleveland?" he asked, defending his pawn with his bishop.

"That he doesn't like me."

"Of course he likes you. He's smitten."

"He is not."

"He most certainly is."

That was not a direction I wanted to go in.

I decided to shake things up a little and moved my pawn so that I was head-to-head with his. He brought his knight beside his bishop and rested. I brought my other little pawn in front of my knight, hoping to set my bishop loose. But his resting knight swung forward, threatening mine. *Uh-oh*, I'd left him unprotected.

But the situation was not dire. I could move my knight into several safe places, including back into its stable, or I could protect him with my bishop or my queen. I opted for my queen's protection because that way I vaguely threatened his knight.

There. He retreated hastily. *Goodbye*.

"Joel didn't like me either." I frowned. "I remember being surprised that he decided to hire me to try to find his daughter even though he disliked me so much. It didn't make sense."

"Like he was accusing you of something?"

"Maybe. I don't really blame Cleveland for imagining there's a con involved."

"It's possible Joel sent instructions to pay you, but the person didn't get the instructions till after he was dead and went ahead anyway."

"Yes, or …"

"Or what?"

"Maybe they transferred the money in spite of the fact he was dead."

"To frame you?"

"Or for distraction. Something that would take the focus off from Wakefield's murder."

I looked up and met his eyes. He seemed to be scrutinizing me with a fiery intensity. But I knew he was hardly aware I was there. His entire concentration was on what was happening inside his head.

Back to my brave bishop. I moved out a square so that he too could attack that pesky pawn.

In return, Leandros's bishop terrorized my queen. I'd better get her to safety fast.

He brought up another little pawn to protect his. I was going to have to sacrifice a knight for two pawns. Was it worth it? He was adept with pawns, I thought, so I decided to go for it.

His queen swooped forward and checked my King. Oh. Now I saw what had happened. My bishop was unprotected and I was in check so my poor bishop was doomed. *Damn*.

I brought it forward to try to intimidate his Queen and protect my King at the same time, but I knew what he was going to do.

He did it.

So now he had my rook and my bishop and I'd only imprisoned two little pawns of his.

Still, *live in hope, die in despair,* I reminded myself. I brought a pawn forward, bravely challenging his arrogant Queen.

Uh-oh. There went my rook. And it looked as though my knight was doomed as well and very possibly I would be in checkmate before I knew it. How had this happened?

Slightly in shock, I pulled myself together. I couldn't lose this early in the game! I moved my pawn forward so that my knight was protected by my valiant queen.

Okay, take my poor little pawn, *go ahead.* I was being slaughtered.

While Leandros contemplated his next move, my eyes focused on his Italian shoes. They were the kind that had little holes punched in around the toe — lace-ups ... maybe they were even Berluti.

I missed the old running shoes he used to wear. He'd changed so much.

Something came back to me. "Why were Joel's shoes brand-new? The soles were actually shiny."

He looked up again. "Do you think that's a clue?"

"I remember thinking it was weird he came to see me with brand new shoes on."

"His secretary might know where he bought them."

"They weren't ordinary shoes. They're like yours. They must've cost hundreds of dollars."

"It's worth looking into, since you noticed them." One thing about Leandros was that he trusted my intuition. He even called me for advice on occasion. "So we have the new shoes, the fact he didn't like you, and that you were paid after he died. Our detective thinks it adds up to some sort of con, and I have to say I agree with him. But who's behind it?"

"I don't know. And will he make me pay back that $5,000? I've spent a quarter of it already—what with the trip to San Francisco."

"We'll have to make sure you get to keep it then." He acted like I was talking about $20.

I brought my queen to threaten his queen; she murdered me, and my King ruthlessly murdered her.

There was blood flowing in the streets.

I knew I should resign at this point. But stubbornness made me determined to play to the bitter end.

I could always hope for a miracle.

I refused to meet his gray-blue eyes, with their laughing, tender, intelligent gleam. He was waiting for me to resign.

I brought my king up to threaten his knight. There wasn't much else I could do. What was he waiting for? *Kill me now—don't let me linger.*

My only hope now was a draw. So I sacrificed my pawn.

He took another pawn and I took it with my pawn. It was ridiculous to hope for a draw but maybe I could trick him into it.

Not very likely. Not with his knight, a bishop, and two rooks. Plus three pawns. And the three pawns who were still left on my side were lined up in train formation and couldn't go anywhere very fast. I couldn't take the pawn that was blocking them because his rook waited menacingly for me to make that move. Even my brave king had very few places to go.

I said out loud. "Okay, I resign."

"That was a good game," he said seriously, and I knew he meant it. He glanced at his watch again. "I'd better get back to the hotel."

I was disappointed that Leandros and Percy didn't have a chance to meet before Leandros went back to California. I wondered what they would think of each other. I could tell that Leandros was impressed by how Percy helped me, but he was also suspicious. I didn't blame him. I'd let a complete stranger into my house, my business, and my life.

"I'm sorry I didn't meet your friend, but you will be on guard around him, won't you?" Leandros cautioned. "I mean, you don't really know who he is or what he's after."

"Maybe Joel isn't even dead, and Percy, the detectives, they're all in this together," I teased as he put on his coat. "Setting me up for a big con."

"Don't say that."

"I'm kidding. I don't have anything worth conning."

"You have a house in the heart of Greenwich Village."

"Percy's okay," I said. "You'll see when you meet him."

Leandros left for his hotel, and then he was off to

the airport. He was one of the most relaxed travelers I've ever known. He allowed plenty of time in transit and so he was never rushed, but it was more than that. He really did look as though he was looking forward to slogging through heavy traffic on the Long Island Expressway and then stuffing himself into a claustrophobic flying can for several hours. Maybe it was different if you were flying first class all the time.

It was the middle of the afternoon, and I felt a sharp lull in energy. Brigitte had texted: she wanted to go see a movie with me; she also wanted to find out how things were going with the sweet boy who fell off my stoop.

I was tempted by the movie idea, and very restless in my empty house. Leandros's departure always did this to me, although I'd never tell him so.

But going out to a movie seemed frivolous. I was still in potentially serious trouble. I declined Brigitte's invitation but my restlessness grew.

Gazing at the chess board that I still hadn't put away, I was struck by the realization that there was one person I still hadn't spoken with, the man who was initially responsible for my involvement in this whole thing from the beginning. The man who Joel Wakefield asked about—he had wanted to know whether he could trust him. Simon Jones.

What did Joel intend to trust him with?

39. Simon Jones lived in Bushwick, in a building that turned out to be at least a fifteen-minute walk from the nearest subway station. The wind whittled my face as I walked, and I was glad when I arrived.

Standing in the shelter of the drab vestibule while I waited to be buzzed inside, I thought that whatever Joel paid him, it wasn't enough.

He didn't ask who it was, just buzzed me inside and leaned over a rickety wooden bannister from the second floor.

"Up here."

I went up the narrow stairs. I'd imagined Simon Jones as a stuffy, fussy, older accountant with neatly dyed hair.

Instead I was greeted by a youngish, blond, thin fellow, in skinny jeans, Converse sneakers, and a ponytail. He had some hairs around his throat and chin, and some on his upper lip, but I couldn't really call it facial hair. More like lint.

He jerked his head, inviting me inside. I smelled incense and heard some kind of soft instrumental new age music.

I perched on the edge of a folded over futon, and he sat cross-legged on the carpet. I saw no reason to hide why I was there and plunged right in. "Joel Wakefield came to see me the day before he was killed. He mentioned your name. He hired me to find his daughter, and he paid me $5,000 to do so."

He regarded me without expression, and sniffed some smoke wafting from the stick incense. I couldn't believe he was really an accountant at an investment firm. "Did you?" he asked.

"Did I what?"

"Find his daughter."

"Yes, I did."

His guileless blue eyes narrowed and he suddenly didn't look so goofy. "Where is she?"

"Why would I tell you?"

His eyes flickered in annoyance, like he was offended, and I wondered if he was part of the cult and there was some weird connection here. But it seemed so unlikely. If Simon Jones knew where Joel's daughter was, why wouldn't he tell him?

"Do you know anything about the payment that was made?" I asked instead. "The thing is, the money was transferred after he was already dead, so the cops think I'm involved in some kind of fraud. Someone paid me—was it you?"

He didn't say anything right away, but I could tell he was nervous and upset, in spite of his bland look.

"Please tell me," I said.

"Yeah, I screwed up. Joel sent the email before he died but I didn't get to it before that afternoon. I didn't know he was dead when I moved the money."

Oh.

That made sense.

"So why haven't you told the police that's what happened?"

"Joel didn't want anyone to know. It was important to him, and I promised I wouldn't say a word to anyone. I said I'd pay the $5,000 as soon as he asked me to. But he wanted it kept a secret."

I was mystified. Why would he want it kept a secret that he'd hired me to find his daughter? Was he embarrassed at hiring an intuitive?

"I need your help in clearing this up for the police," I said. "I can't believe they haven't asked you about this already."

"I can't get any more involved than I already am," he said. "Look, I have a record. It's not a big deal, but I don't need them to find out about it. It might cost me my job."

"A record for what?"

"A drug possession thing." He glared at me defensively. "Just marijuana. It's legal now, anyway, or pretty much. Joel knew about the conviction. He trusted me. He's friends with my mom, and I've known him forever."

"But —"

"He asked me to make this payment and I said I would when I got the invoice. I told the police what I told you: I paid the invoice not knowing that he was dead. I didn't know what it was for."

I did not understand why Joel Wakefield had to be so secretive about paying an intuitive consultant to find his missing daughter, but I certainly could see that Simon Jones was nervous about getting any more involved in the case.

"At least I know how I got the money and that it really did come from Joel. And I did find his daughter, so I do deserve it." I sighed. "You still work for the company?"

"So far."

I got up to go. "You've been very helpful, and I appreciate your candor." I paused. "Would you write down your email address so I can get in touch with you directly? Or do you have a card?"

He grabbed a piece of paper from a notebook and scrawled his email address and his phone number. "I'm better with text than email. I don't check that as often."

I looked at the paper in my hands. Something didn't seem right. It took me a moment to realize what it was.

I set it on the counter in front of him. "Can you write your address too?"

"But you have that."

"Humor me."

He scrawled again, looking annoyed. He kept glancing at his phone, as though he was getting texts that he would like to answer.

I glanced at the piece of paper: my suspicion was confirmed.

I said goodbye graciously, backing into the hall. He closed the door.

On the stairwell as I headed down, I came face to face with my latex fetish lady-friend.

40. "Tiffany!" I said, and affably held out my gloved hand.

I could see she wanted to push past me without stopping, but the way the stairwell was designed made that impossible without me squeezing against the side of the wall.

Which I didn't.

She glared at me without speaking. There was definitely something up.

"Hello," she said, resentfully.

"I wanted to ask you about Joel Wakefield's shoes."

That got her. "What about them?"

"Where did he buy his shoes? He was wearing brand new ones when he came to see me."

She scrunched her pretty pale forehead, puzzled and upset.

"He must have bought them that morning. I thought since you handled his appointments, you might know."

"Why does it matter?"

"I'm not sure. Did he have a regular store where he bought shoes?"

"Yes; Barney's." She paused. "Actually, he asked me to buy that pair for him. He was busy in meetings all morning, but he needed the shoes for an appointment. I went out and got them for him, but he forgot to give me his credit card. So I paid with mine."

"I see."

"I left the shoes and the receipt on his desk and then I went out for lunch. He wasn't there when I came back. His old shoes were gone too. I never saw him again." Her eyes welled up.

"Okay—that's okay."

"I never got reimbursed."

"Maybe you could arrange that with his estate."

She shook her head, obviously wanting to pass. She'd given me more information than I'd hoped for, so I said goodbye and let her go by, then went on down the stairs and forged my way outside.

The wind had picked up and I clutched my cloak tighter as I struggled through it to the distant subway.

Frozen shreds began fluttering from the white sky. I hadn't checked the weather in a few days, so I didn't know if a storm was heading our way.

I wondered where Percy was.

With relief, I reached the subway, grateful to be out of the wind in spite of the stale chilliness from the tracks. There was no reception so I couldn't call Percy.

A while later I emerged at the West Fourth Street station and hurried along the growing slickness to the supermarket where I picked up vegetables, noodles, cheeses, and some olives, trying to think of what Percy might like to eat.

When I reached my house, I noticed that although my stoop was thinly shrouded with snow, it looked as though a lot of people had gone up and down the steps. Curious about the visitors, I inserted the key in the lock, and entered.

Inside, I was greeted by the sight of Percy seated behind the desk, talking to someone who was standing in front of it. Both chairs had strangers sitting in them, and they looked up in anticipation, as though they were *waiting* for me.

Hiding my surprise, a smart thing to do if you want to convey that you're intuitive, I hung up my cloak, dusting the flakes off first so they didn't soak through. I smiled warmly at the strangers went inside my office, and set down the groceries. I only had to wait a minute before Percy hobbled in on his crutches and closed the door.

"What's going on?" I asked.

"I put an ad in one of the local freebies papers, and said that walk-ins are welcome. So these folks walked in. I didn't realize you were going to be out all afternoon."

"You mean they're all here for consultations?"

He nodded, as though unsure of my reaction. "I told them we could make an appointment for tomorrow, since I didn't know when you'd be free, but they wanted to wait." He eyed me uncertainly, then added: "I suggested to them that they opt for the half-hour introduction for half price. That way you can fit them all in this afternoon. If they want longer appointments, they can book those either through me or through a calendar I set up on your website. They pay when they sign up."

I was so surprised at the thought that I already had two clients waiting for me in the reception area, I was speechless.

"Are you okay?" Percy asked.

I took a deep breath and pulled myself together. "I'm definitely okay."

41.

I was busy till six, and then I had to dash out for my engagement with Judy, which I had missed the week before. I stopped at the market again, this time to pick up flowers, lots of oranges and grapefruits, and a fresh loaf of bread.

Judy was glad to see me, and I was just as happy to see her. Being with her always lifted my spirits. We had met a long time ago, and hadn't always been so close, but when I moved to New York last fall we met up again through a mutual friend, and I made a commitment to spending regular time with her. Sometimes I talked to her about what I was up to, but most of the time she did the talking, quoting Pema Chodron or the Dalai Lama, or telling stories about her childhood.

I stayed longer than usual, because I wanted to tell her why I hadn't been able to come the previous Saturday and about Percy. I described the accident and how he had offered to help me build my business.

"I already have two regular clients signed on for

weekly sessions," I finished.

"Bring him next time you come," her sweet eyes twinkled. "I'd like to meet him."

"We'll have to wait till his ankle is better. Walking isn't easy for him yet."

"Bring him in a taxi."

I realized she had all sorts of romantic notions in her head and quickly set her straight. "He's just a business associate," I said.

She was disappointed that our relationship wasn't more amorous, so I cheered her by promising to bring him to meet her one day soon.

Talking about Percy reminded me that I still hadn't told him about my encounter with Simon Jones and I left soon afterward. The temperature had plummeted, and the piercing arctic squall felt like a cleaver. When I got back, Percy was still in the office, sitting at his desk, his leg on the ottoman, his laptop propped on his thigh. The screen was dark, so I knew he wasn't working.

His face lit up when he saw me. I hastily shut the door against the deep freeze outside, shuddering.

"Hey."

"Brrr."

"I know."

"Percy, it's eight o'clock. Why don't you call it a day and relax? Have you eaten?"

"Yep."

"What did you have?"

"Peanut-butter-and-jelly. Good."

I was surprised myself at how glad I was to see him. "Come on, let's go downstairs to your apartment and I'll see what I can make for you. You need vegetables. Get your crutches—I'll carry your laptop."

We went out the back door, along the stone path, down three steps, which he managed awkwardly. It was bitterly cold out, and I didn't like it. I hadn't thought I'd need my cloak for such a short time outside, but I regretted leaving it inside now. The wind was like a machete, even in this enclosed little garden.

I was glad to get into the warmth of his apartment. I whipped up a stir-fry, using the broccoli, potatoes, and sprouts I'd bought earlier, and while I was cooking I told him about my visit to Simon Jones and the unexpected encounter with Tiffany.

"I have a feeling they're sleeping together. They're obviously close."

I brought him his food, excited to tell him what I discovered. I waited till I had his attention again, then pulled out the piece of paper Simon had written his address on. "Look: loops, and the a's aren't closed."

He looked at me blankly, then shoved another bite into his mouth. "So?"

"The writing sample Joel showed me isn't Simon's! Look." I pointed to the lettering. "This is obviously the writing of an optimist. Joel's sample was sloping way down off the page. The writer was seriously depressed."

"So whose writing was it?"

"I'm not sure yet."

He lifted his fork. "Detective Cleveland dropped

by while you were gone."

"What did he want?"

"He didn't say."

"Should I call back?"

"Tomorrow."

"At least I can't be blamed for Joel's murder. We were together when it happened. You're my alibi."

"Of course."

"Although, he might say that I easily could have slipped out for an hour while you were high on Percocet."

He grinned. "True."

"Seriously, where do we go from here? I don't want to talk to that detective again before I know who killed Joel Wakefield."

"Are you going to tell him about your meeting with Jones?"

"I promised Jones I wouldn't unless I absolutely had to."

Percy finished his plate of stir-fry and I gave him some more. "I had another idea. The half-brother in Hawaii."

"John Henry? What about him?"

"He might have had a motive to kill his brother. You told me they had a big fight in December. That's not so long ago."

"But what would they fight about?"

"It might be a good idea to try to find out. If the fight had something to do with Ruby, is it possible that she might be in danger now?"

I didn't like thinking that Ruby might be in danger. She seemed so vulnerable.

"I can't bear the thought that she might be in danger. What can we do? I can't just fly to Hawaii, break into his house, and find out whether he hired someone to kill his half-brother."

"Why not?" said Percy. "There's still money left over from the $5,000. If you're so worried about her, go ahead and use it."

42.

The first thing I noticed when I got off the plane at the Honolulu airport was the breeze. Normally, I didn't like wind, it made me itchy. But this wind was completely different to anything I'd ever felt before. I sensed immediately its sweetness, its softness, its *aliveness*.

Even walking through the airport, I could feel it through the open walls. I was so happy to be out of the frigid northeast that I felt as though I were walking on some magical frond of colorful air. Everywhere I looked I saw enormous hibiscus, bougainvillea, fragrant pikake.

The hotel where Percy had made a reservation at turned out to be a skyscraper, set back a few streets from the beach. I parked my rental car in its garage, and was shown to a large airy room with a balcony overlooking the glittering bay of Waikiki. The distinctive crown of Diamond Head rose up in the east on my left.

If only Leandros were here, I would be in heaven.

But he was not and that was just as well. I needed to focus on the task at hand, which was getting in touch with John Henry. I showered, changed, and went out to the terrace to watch the sun set and to text Percy.

What now? I asked him.

He called me instead of texting.

"Tomorrow's a work week. John Henry will be going to his office. When you see him leave, get inside his house and find his laptop. I'm sure he doesn't take it with him. He lives alone so there won't be anyone else there."

"How do I break into his house?"

"As long as he doesn't have a dog, I can help you figure out a way. If you hear a dog, then you'll have to go to his office instead."

"What am I looking for?"

"Some link to Joel Wakefield—something recent. Maybe an email, maybe a document or a spreadsheet. You have the data stick I gave you, right?"

"Yes."

"If you can't find anything quickly, just copy everything you can onto that stick and I'll check it out. Easy."

I couldn't imagine it was going to be easy breaking into a stranger's house, much less digging through his personal computer files, but thinking about Ruby gave me courage. I was certain that the fact that Joel wanted me to find his daughter, and then he had died, was related in some way.

What if Ruby were in danger herself? Was that what her mother was afraid of, and why she wanted her safe in the commune?

"Okay. What should I do this evening? It's still early."

"Have fun."

"I feel I should be working."

"You are—in your own way. Besides, I'll bet you'll be up way before dawn. Jet lag."

So I walked the beach, my flip-flops in my hands and my toes in the warm ocean. There were plenty of people around, enjoying the balmy serenity, some even swimming in the moonlit ocean.

Eventually I stopped at an outdoor table at one of the hotel restaurants and ordered a mai tai. Tiki torches were alight all around me. Twice I was approached by someone asking whether they could join me or buy me a drink, but I declined.

Later, sitting on the hotel room terrace, I looked out at the moon smoking high above in a sea of faint cloud and stars. In the northeast, especially in winter, the moon seemed cold and distant. Here she was like the smiling face of a goddess, floating, sipping, warm. I felt suspended in silvery vibrations that had condensed and solidified, to create a real, tangible world. I sensed the thousands of miles of ocean surrounding and pulling me deep into its soul, and then summoning me into a vortex of watery light toward the sky.

I felt that with the slightest tremble, the mysterious vibrations could turn into ghosts and elementals and other-worldly experiences.

I was far too excited to sleep.

43.

The address Percy gave me was in a small town on the windward side of the island. In the pitch dark of early morning, a valet brought my car to the hotel entrance. I set off with a map on the seat beside me, circling around Diamond Head toward Waimanalo.

It was still dark when I stopped for take-out coffee in the center of Kailua, and studied the map on my phone. John Henry's house was on a bland-looking cul-de-sac that anywhere else would be merely decent, but here was probably worth over a million dollars.

The sun looked as though it might never show up. I was so wide awake the darkness felt peculiar, until I reminded myself that it was nearing noon back in the east.

I parked on the opposite side of the street from John Henry's house, about fifty feet from his driveway. Then I sipped coffee, and waited. John Henry was probably still asleep.

The morning sky grew light with sudden enthusiasm. The brightness of the sun struck the dark green tops of the lava crags, and the wind-tossed coconut trees behind the houses. I was so used to the gradual twilight of the northeast that it took me a moment to adjust.

After a while the garage door of John Henry's house slid up. A sporty sedan slipped down the drive and turned left, hardly pausing to check for oncoming traffic. I guess he was late for work.

He passed by much too quickly for me to recognize him from the blurry photograph Percy had texted me.

The garage door closed by itself.

I called Percy. "He's gone. Drove off. Are you sure he doesn't live with anyone?"

"Positive," Percy said confidently.

"How do I get in? Looks like security protection everywhere."

"Hear a dog?"

"No."

"Then walk up to the front door and knock."

With my cell phone in the crook of my neck, I followed Percy's instructions. I was too nervous to think straight.

No one answered my knock.

"What do I do now?" I asked. "I can't break a window."

Percy chuckled. "Of course not. Walk around the side of the house and find a door where you can't be seen from the street. I'm going to teach you a trick."

I skulked along the side of the house and felt better when I turned the corner and found myself in a small backyard.

"I'm at the side door."

"Take out your hotel key. I know this is going sound tricky, but it's really not. Now, hold it vertically. Slide it into the side of the door, where the lock is."

I took out the card and did as he instructed.

"Got it."

"Okay," he said. "The doorjamb is opposite the door and is the part that the lock goes into. Insert the card as far as it will go at a perpendicular angle with the door. Push the door back as far as it can go with your other hand so you can see where the door jamb is."

"Okay."

"What happens when you do that?"

"Nothing."

"Then tilt the card toward the doorknob. Now push in slightly—does it slide in a little more?"

"No."

"Try it again. Tilt the card till it's even touching the doorknob. You're just getting the card into place by the bolt so you can push it back down."

"Really?" I am doubtful.

"Trust me. This will work. The only reason it won't is if he's got deadbolts, like you do at your house."

"I'm glad I do, if this trick works."

"Now, bend the card the opposite way. This will make the card slip under the angled end of the bolt. Jiggle it a bit."

"Nothing happens."

"Did you hear anything?"

"A sort of click."

"Try it again and as soon as you hear the click, push on the door. In fact, try leaning against the door while you do it; it might help it to pop open. You can also continue to wiggle and jiggle the door back and forth as you shift the card. Try it again."

I did.

Abruptly, the door flew open.

"I'm in!" I whispered.

I was in a neat living room with wicker furniture. There was a hall leading to a sunny garden in the back and several closed doors.

"Good. Now see if there's some kind of an office where he keeps his laptop."

I tiptoed on the wall-to-wall carpet to the first door, which turned out to be a large kitchen and dining room that smelled strongly of stale weed. Across from it was the den. A laptop sat on top of a messy desk, piled high with papers, books, and bills.

"Found it," I whispered. "He's a slob."

"Open the laptop."

"It's already open."

"Then stick the drive I gave you in the USB port."

I found the port, shoved in the drive, and waited for it to show up on the screen.

"Okay, it's on the screen."

"Try copying his documents onto the drive. Skip any photos. Shouldn't take too long."

I waited with bated breath as I copied the files— mostly spreadsheets—onto the drive.

While I waited, I opened the top desk drawer. It was filled with the usual boxes of paperclips, rubber-bands, pens, and white-out. The one below it was for hanging file folders. I rifled through the headings until I saw it: Joel Wakefield.

Hastily, I pulled it out and opened it. The computer files were still being copied, so I had time.

"I found a file with some sort of insurance policy," I whispered to Percy, who was still on the phone.

"What kind of insurance?"

"Not sure." I thumbed through the papers till I came across Joel Wakefield's signature.

And stared.

I had never seen it before. But I recognized the writing.

Then, from somewhere else in the house, I heard the sound of the toilet flushing. My heart in my throat, I whispered, "There's somebody else here."

"Don't panic," said Percy, which immediately made me panic.

"What should I do?" I hissed.

"Pull out the drive and put it in your purse. Don't worry about waiting to eject. Grab it, now."

My mind a crazy blur of terror, I pulled out the drive and shoved it in my bra. Then I quickly closed the lid of the laptop, hoping that would get rid of the evidence.

The manila file was still open in front of me, and I shoved it back in the drawer and closed it.

Images of being thrown into a Honolulu jail rose up like an enormous wave. I'd broken into someone's home! I'd stolen files!

What was Percy thinking?

What was *I* thinking?

Could I escape?

I heard steps coming down the hall and the panic rose.

I held my breath as the footsteps neared.

44.

A young woman slouched into the doorway and gaped at me. Maybe she was eighteen, but if so it happened recently. I could tell she had been out late last night; she hadn't washed off her make-up and her hair still had sticky spray in it. I also was sure she'd been crying recently. Maybe a fight with her boyfriend? She wore a baggy men's t-shirt, which I assumed was John Henry's. So she was somehow involved with him.

She was also high and dissipated, and unsurprised to see me there.

"Who are you?" she slurred, leaning against the door jam.

She sounded suspicious and despairing, but I knew it was not because she'd caught me rifling through her boyfriend's desk, but because she felt jealous.

I summoned my sleight of mouth. "Hi. John Henry sent me here to pick up something he needs at the office. I'm an assistant."

The Voice worked like magic, and she even gave

me a tentative smile.

I smiled back. "How are you doing today? Have you had breakfast yet?" My Voice was relaxed, reassuring. As I moved cautiously from behind the desk, I subtly mirrored her drooping posture so she'd sense a rapport.

"I'll be going now. Take care of yourself."

I eased past her into the hall, threw back the bolts on the front door, and stepped out into the front yard.

The sun was high in the bright blue sky and there wasn't a soul in sight. Trying not to run, I hurried to my car, clutching my phone and purse. Not too fast, not too slow. I got in, nervously checked the back seat—empty. I closed the door, buckled up.

I was so jittery I could hardly put the key into the ignition.

It was not until I'd gone several blocks that I realized my phone was still on and I could hear Percy's voice begging me to tell him whether or not I was okay. I picked up the phone and pressed speaker.

"I think so—but I really want to get out of here and I'm not sure of directions. I'll call you back."

"Don't hang up!" he yelled. "I can help. Give me a landmark."

I drove faster than I should, anxious to get as far away as possible before the young woman roused herself enough to call the police. I tried to notice signs once I was on the highway but all I saw was that the ocean was on my right and the mountains on my left.

"Then you're heading toward the North Shore," Percy told me. "You need to turn around and go back to your hotel."

There was nowhere to turn. I kept driving until I was on a road that coasted a wide beach. There was a hunched-over island not too far offshore. I described where I was to Percy.

"Keep heading north. You can get back to Waikiki from the North Shore by cutting through the middle of the island."

That sounded fine to me. Now the adrenalin rushed in and I was on a high of excitement.

"So what's next?"

"Send me the contents of the flash drive when you get back to the hotel."

"Should I try to talk to John Henry in person?"

"Maybe."

"I want to ask him about that insurance I found. But won't he be suspicious?"

Percy laughed. "Suspicious of what? You're not accusing him and you're not defending yourself. Relax. You're investigating."

I smiled. "I guess I've never done this investigation thing before."

"You're a natural," he assured me. "Anyway, I think you do it every day, when you do your consultations. You're investigating, following trains of thought, discovering, and then piecing it all together."

My heart lifted again, and it wasn't the adrenalin this time. The blue sky, the unfamiliar freshly-carved mountains that reared up into the bright sunshine, delighted me.

"Let me know when you're back at the hotel, okay?" Percy said. "Or call if you get lost and your phone's not giving you proper directions."

I lingered for a while on a wide beach where the waves were high as houses. I didn't swim—I was not good with heights and those waves were breathtaking enough seen from the shore. Instead I watched the brave surfers crouch, and leap, and whirl, and teeter and burst into the foamy spray, and then I waited in interminable suspense for them to re-emerge.

I was back at my hotel by mid-afternoon. I shoved the data stick into my laptop and started sending the files to Percy, glancing at them as they scrolled past me, wondering if I would get some sort of feeling about any of them.

Instead, I ended up dozing. My sleepless night had kicked in.

I was woken by my cell. It was Percy.

"Hey—I think we found something interesting."

I sat up, groggy. "We did?"

"Yep. Joel sent an email to John Henry telling him that he hired you to find Ruby. Says he could trust you and that he's sure you'll be successful. Want me to read it?"

"Sure."

"'Satyana's a psychic and she has agreed to track down Ruby, so if you still don't have any luck, follow up with her. You can trust her—she's smart, she's stunning, and ...'"

I interrupted, blushing. "Okay. Is that all?"

I heard the chuckle in his voice. "Something even better. Looks like Joel Wakefield asked John Henry to get a life insurance policy out on him."

Aha.

"For one million dollars. He got it in early December. And guess who the beneficiary is?"

I didn't have to guess.

I already knew.

Ruby.

45.

"Oh my God," I said. "Do you think he knew he was going to die? That's why he wanted me to find Ruby?"

"I don't know. But I do think you need to talk to John Henry. He needs to know where she is, so he can tell her she's the beneficiary. Right?"

"I guess so. What if he doesn't want to see me?"

"Try."

He texted me John Henry's phone number again and I texted John Henry. *"This is Sati. I knew your brother. I'm in Hawaii—can we meet?"*

I received a text back from John Henry almost immediately. *OK—which hotel are you at?*

We agreed to meet in the lobby at six and I hopped into the shower since it was already nearing that time. My little black dress, which was always just right in New York, seemed ridiculously gloomy here. I opted for an orange sundress and sandals.

I was putting on some lipstick when I heard a knock on the door. I went over and peered out the peephole. A stocky man with a hairpiece, wearing a flamboyant Hawaiian shirt, was waiting impatiently.

"Yes?" I called through the door.

"John Henry."

Uh-oh. I didn't want to be rude, but we had agreed to meet in the bar. I didn't want him inside my room.

Sure I snooped on his computer, but I don't *know* this guy.

"Be right there."

I quickly put on my cream gloves, picked up my shawl and purse, made sure my card key was inside, and stepped out into the hall. I closed the door behind me quickly.

I couldn't help it—this guy made me nervous.

He was hovering close, but stepped back at my abruptness. The long hallway was empty and quiet.

I pretended I was fine. "I'm Satyana. So nice to meet you."

John Henry had a square face and a small nose, and the hair he'd selected looked oddly pale against his tan. The shirt was decorated with large guitars and leis. He'd recently bought new eyeglasses; I could tell, because the indents his old ones made were clearly visible just a few centimeters beneath the new ones. These were nice. The sandals were good leather too, and looked new. I wondered whether he'd recently come into some money.

He touched a glove with his middle finger and smirked. "Fashion statement or a germ issue?"

Right away I did not like him. I did not like the fact that he came all the way up to my hotel room instead of meeting at the bar. I did not like him knowing which room I was in. The plastic card key in my purse seemed particularly flimsy when I thought how easy it had been to break into his house.

Had that young woman told him I was there?

"Neither," I said.

"Or maybe both?"

I liked him even less.

We entered the elevator and he said blandly, but with an undercurrent of rage that frightened me: "So, what were you doing in my house this morning? What were you looking for?"

I know immediately that it was important to use the Voice with John Henry. If I didn't, he was likely to turn me into the police. He was *furious* under that cheerful shirt and deep tan. It was only curiosity that had gotten him to meet me.

Or … maybe he did not want to involve the police unless he had to.

If the young woman who was in his house was under eighteen, that could be a reason for secrecy. But I had a feeling there was another reason.

As we swooshed down in the elevator, I used my most coaxing and reassuring Voice.

"Look, I'm in a bind. I met your brother the day before he was killed, and the cops think I may have something to do with it."

He didn't buy it. "Why?"

The elevator doors opened onto the lobby, and there was too much noise for my Voice to be effective. I decided to wait till we were seated at a small booth in the lobby bar. I would have preferred to be outside at one of the vibrant places on the beach, with tiki torches blazing, and slide guitars and ukeles serenading me, the sun setting over thousands of miles of deep water. But John Henry didn't want to leave the hotel. For him, this was just business, and he wanted to get it over with.

I ordered a glass of champagne. I'd already spent so much money on this wild caper, I figured I might as well. The $5,000 must be pretty well depleted by now.

He had a beer. "Go on."

"Someone transferred $5,000 into my PayPal from your brother's account, soon after he died. I'm just trying to talk to anyone who might be able to help figure out who did it and why."

The Voice was starting to take effect. I could see his hard eyes begin to show a flicker of sympathy. Then it vanished. "I haven't seen my brother in two years."

"Oh." I sip the bubbles and they go up my nose. "I thought he came to see you in December. He was here, wasn't he?"

He looked annoyed. "I didn't see him, I just told you that."

I frowned. Why was he lying?

Who was he protecting?

"I happen to know that you took out a one million dollar life insurance on your brother last month. So you must have seen him."

He sneered. "I don't have to see a client to buy an insurance policy for him."

"So you did get that insurance for him?"

He was silent, exuding hostility and resentment. But he didn't argue or get defensive. Something else was going on.

"His daughter's the beneficiary, right?" I persisted. "Is that why Joel wanted me to find her? Did he know he was going to die?"

John Henry neared me, getting right in my face. "Look, stay out of this, will you? You don't know what you're getting mixed up in. This is not some pretty girl game you're playing, you weird mystic psycho. Stay out of what you don't understand. Get the hell away from us all."

He threw a ten-dollar bill on the counter—which barely covered his beer—and stormed out.

I remained where I was. I was starting to piece it together. Very slowly, it was starting to come to me, like the strains of a violin from some far-off place in a dark forest.

He was protecting someone.

Ruby?

Or—

I paid too and wandered outside. It wasn't yet eight o'clock, so Kalakaua surged with tourists. I headed toward the beach, longing to call Percy but not wanting to wake him. The moon was big and full, pouring silver into the folds of satin ocean below. The silky breeze stroked me, like a gentle hand.

It took a long time, sitting there and watching the

moon flow up through the large stars, before it all began to make sense.

John Henry didn't kill his brother, and nor did Ruby.

They were both *protecting* him.

But from what? From whom?

Why would they be protecting someone who was already dead?

46. My plane had a stopover in Los Angeles and Leandros drove to LAX to take me out for lunch. I only had a few hours between flights, and since the airport restaurant was closed, he drove me farther afield but promised to return in time to get me through security again.

I didn't usually enjoy seeing Leandros in Los Angeles, since it was his turf and I felt out of place. But I wanted to talk to him about my meeting with John Henry. He took me to a small place near the marina and I told him what I'd discovered during my trip.

"Joel Wakefield took out an insurance policy for his half-brother for one million dollars. His daughter, Ruby, gets all of it."

"There's motive for murder. I don't know why you're so convinced the girl is innocent. That's an okay sum to kill for."

"No, she didn't do it. I doubt she even knows about the policy."

"You seem to really like her."

"Yes, I do. She's had some unlucky breaks but there's something about her..."

I watched his long, square-tipped fingers tap his glass. His eyes were narrow, focused on the ice as though it was the most interesting thing in the world.

I knew he didn't even see it. It was a knack he had, so that people thought he was concentrating on them when he was actually miles away. I knew he was onto something.

Yes, he had an idea. He looked up.

"The cult? Did someone there find out about Ruby's potential insurance inheritance?"

"It's possible. And they're hoping she'll give the money to them? It seems awfully risky. Besides, it's not as though Twang is hard-up or about to go bankrupt. And he's already had enough bad publicity last year—remember that sex scandal? Being accused of murder, even if it can't be proved, would be nuts for the goldmine he's got going there."

"Greed makes people nutty."

"I get the feeling he's more greedy for power than for money."

"Money is power."

He had ordered me a sparkling wine and it was going to my head because of sleeplessness and excitement. I picked at the caprese salad, and bit into a plump caper.

"What if she were convicted—who would inherit?"

"Maybe her mother?"

I thought that one over. Would her mother plan such an elaborate scheme to inherit her ex-husband's life insurance?

"He was paying her alimony, not only child support. It would be like killing the golden goose."

"But Wakefield's investments weren't too solid," he told me. "The company he was most invested in was about to go bankrupt. Remember, I told you Wolcott Candies is about to file for bankruptcy? If he'd lived, he'd be ruined."

I remembered. "Do you think he knew about that?"

"He must have."

We looked at each other.

"So there was no money there, except in the insurance policy," I said.

"That's right."

"Then I think I have it."

"What?"

"The shoes."

"Shoes?"

"Yes!" It was so clear to me, I couldn't believe I hadn't realized before. "Why would he want people to know he'd bought a brand new pair of shoes?"

"Makes no sense."

"Yes, it does. And you know what? It was *his* writing he'd asked me to analyze when he came to me. I figured that out when I saw his signature. That meant *he* was the one who was depressed…"

Leandros shook his head. "Sati, he was murdered, in plain sight, with dozens of witnesses. It couldn't have been suicide."

I was so excited I was practically bouncing in my chair. "He wanted it to look like it wasn't! That's why he bought new shoes…he didn't care if they fit well or not!"

"I see…"

"That's why he had his secretary buy them! He wanted people to think he was fine—he wanted there to be no shadow of a doubt that he was murdered."

"His secretary bought the shoes?"

"Yes!" I told him about meeting up with Tiffany. "Know what I think? I think that insurance policy has a clause that exempts the company from paying on suicide. Many do. And he wanted to be sure his daughter got all the money."

"But…"

"That's why everyone we know has an alibi. No one killed him."

Leandros still didn't buy it. "He *was* murdered, my dear Sati. There *were* witnesses. Cleveland doesn't have the imagination to make that up."

"I know. But don't you get it? He hired someone to do it. Joel Wakefield *wanted* to die."

47. Instead of getting on my scheduled flight to New York, I changed my plans. I knew I was in no way related to Ruby, and we were not even friends. But in asking me to find her, Joel Wakefield had linked us. I felt responsible for her now.

I called Percy to let him know I was going to make a detour to San Francisco. "I'm going to make a plea to Twang to let Ruby go. It'll just be a brief layover. I'll take the red-eye from there and be home in the morning."

"Detective Cleveland's come by twice already, looking for you."

"What's he want?"

"Something's come up. He won't say what."

"Tell him I'll be back tomorrow. I have some news for him too."

Percy really didn't want me to go, but my flight was boarding and there was nothing he could do about it.

This time I took a taxi to the Twang-Doh commune. When I showed up at the door of the Spanish-style stucco mansion, the woman who gave me the tour the first time I was here greeted me with that same guarded smile.

I asked her if I could see Twang.

"Tell him I know a friend of his, Joel Wakefield,"

I said, using my most confident Voice.

She could shut the door in my face, I knew that. On the other hand, curiosity is usually more powerful than fear.

She was definitely curious. She let me inside, and I waited in the lounge that smelled of sandalwood and lentils. From another part of the mansion I heard distant chanting and I wondered how Ruby was.

Twenty minutes passed before another woman entered and nodded at me. "This way, please."

I followed her along a terra-cotta hallway, up tiled stairs, into a spacious room with rich red cherry floors. Twang—I assumed it was him—was seated in a lotus position on an ottoman, the light from the large windows behind him. It was often my experience that religious and spiritual leaders liked to sit with the light behind them. I figured they thought it gave them a look of mystery and other-worldliness. Without the sunshine exposing a pimple or an irritated look, these leaders could pretend more power than they have. It's a Wizard of Oz trick.

Twang had a round face and a round belly. He wore a lavender cotton shirt and baggy white trousers and his back was straight as a pencil. Hs eyes twinkled. His skin was a pleasant milk chocolate color, and his hair black as crow feathers. It looked dyed.

There were plenty of other people in the room. That surprised me, because I thought he would want to meet with me privately. But he didn't. The others were casually seated on floor pillows or folded blankets, their eyes closed or devotedly focused on

Twang. They seemed hardly to notice me, as though I was a cat that wandered in or a leaf blown by the wind.

I was ushered to a burgundy cushion near Twang's knee. I didn't like the idea of being on a lower level than this cult leader, so I ignored the cushion and smiled politely down at the master.

Smiling back, he unlaced his legs, and stood too. He was shorter and softer than I expected. I tried not to imagine him with Ruby.

He ogled me as though he really admired me and reached out to take my gloved hand in his.

"I understand Joel was your friend," he said in a sonorous voice. There wasn't the trace of a foreign accent.

"Yes, he was, and Ruby is too. Joel was murdered, you know. But before he died, he asked me to take care of Ruby." I hoped he wouldn't intuit my half-lie. "I promised I would. I take my promises seriously."

Still holding my hand, he graciously guided me to the large bay window, away from his nearest enthusiast. Situating himself again with the sunlight behind him, he nodded up at me. "I never met Joel, you know."

I extricated my hand.

"Did you know that Ruby was going to be a rich woman if he died?"

His eyes widened. "No, I did not."

Liar.

Again he took my gloved hand in his and stroked it. He leaned in toward me.

"You think I am lying, but I speak the truth. We are alike, you and I. We want to help people. I want to help Ruby. She has suffered in her past, and here she has begun to heal. We mustn't remove her too soon."

I removed my hand. "I think she is ready to be removed. The only reason you won't let her go is if you think you're going to get some of her money. And I'm here to let you know that I'll make damn sure you don't get a penny."

He tut-tutted, looking disappointed in me. "We do only good here, Satyana. Anyone is free to come and to go—ask anyone. We offer community service and spiritual individual practice. It is only for the good. It is only about love."

I was tempted to ask him about his teachings about sex, but knew I couldn't change the world.

All I could do was change one small part of it.

"If that's true, then let Ruby go. Send her home where she belongs. She needs to finish college and live her own life."

"You don't understand." He sighed deeply. "She *wants* to be here."

"You can make it so she doesn't want to be here. You know it's up to you."

I could see him wrestling inwardly. He didn't want to admit that he had this kind of power over his disciples, because he knew I saw through him. On the other hand, he wanted nothing to do with the scandal of Joel's death.

"It's really not up to me…" he murmured.

"I said I will do everything in my power to free

her, and I will. I'm going to make sure she gets out of here and forges her own life on her own terms, not yours. No matter what it takes. That means I *will* involve you in the police investigation surrounding her father's death. I *will* involve you in the relationship you have with Ruby. After what you went through last year, do you really want to go through that again? Let her go."

He muttered something, shook his head gloomily. "You don't understand. It's not that I wish for her money…"

"Ah, so you do know about her money, and you're hoping to get at least some of it?"

"No."

"Then why not let her go?"

We stared at each other. I saw in his soft eyes a yearning, as though he longed for more of something he could not have.

I spoke the words I knew he needed to hear.

"If it's not about the money, then it's about power. I understand. But you have the power, that's what I'm telling you. *Now* is when your power is strongest. Ruby admires you—she'll do what you say." I pressed the point home. "But do you think she'll still see you as powerful after another court drama like the one you went through before? Do you think lawyers and judges won't open her eyes to the truth of who you actually are? You have sex with her, for God's sake!"

"She is a grown-up. It is part of her healing."

"You know that's not true." I raised my voice and some of the people nearest to us looked over in surprise. "Sex with a guru like yourself is a power-play. It's abuse."

"Now—now—" he smiled, but his eyes were tense. "You don't know what you're talking about."

"You know damn well I do." My return smile wasn't tense in the least—it was dangerous. "You're an intelligent man. You are powerful, I grant that. But you know you can't win this time. You can't keep her. I won't allow it. Set her free. Send her back where she belongs."

48.

My red-eye was delayed and I didn't get back to New York till after eight the next morning. When I entered my house, I found Detective Cleveland seated in one of the super-comfortable scissor chairs, staring at his heavy black boots. Percy was behind the desk, one leg propped on the ottoman, working on his laptop.

He looked up in relief when I came in, and so did Detective Cleveland.

"Good morning!" I dropped my tote, hung up my cloak, and went over to Percy first. "Everything okay? Any clients scheduled?"

"Not till ten," he said, looking really glad to see me. "And another one this afternoon at three."

I turned to the detective. "Thanks for stopping

by."

He scowled. "Humph."

I was actually starting to like him, in spite of his restless irritation. That's what happens when something gets to be familiar, and he certainly was that by now.

"Coffee?" I offered him cheerfully.

"No, thanks. I need to talk to you."

"Then come inside my office," I invited. "I have lots to tell you."

I knew Percy would want to hear what I had to say, so I left the door open between us. I sat in the burnt orange velvet swivel chair and motioned Detective Cleveland to the settee.

"You first," I smiled.

"I thought you'd want to know we've arrested the man who killed Joel Wakefield."

I was enormously relieved to hear that. "Congratulations! Who is he?"

"His name is Becker. Joe Becker. He admitted he never met Joel Wakefield, but he was hired to kill him."

I nodded.

"Becker claims his client promised $10,000 for the hit. Half up front, and $5,000 at completion."

I heard shuffling in the other room, and knew Percy was listening intently.

"Do you know who his client was?" I asked.

"Not yet—but we're getting closer."

I was about to jump in, but he went on, marking off various points on his thick fingers.

"We know his accountant, Simon Jones, paid

your invoice. Apparently, he'd been given instructions to pay $5,000 to a person who was going to contact him in the next few days. Your invoice showed up and he paid it without checking first. Wakefield was already dead, although Jones hadn't heard that news yet. Of course, Becker was not going to send an invoice via PayPal. When he contacted Jones by phone just an hour later, Jones said he'd already paid the invoice via PayPal. He gave Becker your name. That's why Becker threatened you—he thought you'd found out about the money he was owed and you stole it from him."

"That sounds like what happened."

"So, he went after you to get the money that Simon Jones accidentally put into your account."

"Not accidentally!" I protested. "I charged Joel Wakefield to find his missing daughter, and I found her. I earned every penny."

He looked at me skeptically. "Sure you did." He sighed, his eyebrows lowering over his eyes. "Trouble is, we still don't know who hired Becker to murder Wakefield. Becker says he doesn't know either, and I think he's telling the truth."

"Ah—but I know," I said.

The detective pushed up the heavy eyebrows and stared. "What? Who?"

I heard Percy's crutches on the floor. Of course he would want to hear this too. I waited till he was leaning against the door jamb, gazing at me with a glint of admiration.

I met his eyes.

"Joel Wakefield himself."

"Of course!" Percy breathed.

I could practically see his mind bounding ahead to piece together the whole picture.

The detective was slower on the uptake. He grunted, "Why would he do that?"

"Suicide."

"There are much simpler ways. Why not jump out a window?"

"Because he didn't want anyone to think it was suicide."

Percy nodded. Cleveland glanced at him uncertainly, and nodded as well. "Okay, even if I buy it, why?"

"Because he took out a one million dollar life insurance policy a month ago. We found that out from his half-brother who works for an insurance company. They had an argument—I'm pretty sure that his brother knew why he wanted the life insurance and was trying to talk him out of it. They had a big fight over it, but he went ahead anyway."

Percy broke in, excitedly. "Of course! And the life insurance policy doesn't cover suicide—is that it?"

"That's it. He had to figure out a way to die that wouldn't look like suicide. That's when he put this plan into action. I bet when you ask Becker, he'll tell you that Joel contacted him for the first time a month ago. I bet that's when he paid him the first half of the contract."

Detective Cleveland grunted. "Why did he want to kill himself?"

"He knew he would lose everything when Wolcott Candies went under," I said. "He was totally invested in that company. He'd be not just broke but hugely in debt. And he couldn't face it." I took a breath. "And he also wanted to make absolutely sure his daughter was taken care of."

"But now we know that Wakefield killed himself, does that mean the girl won't get any of that insurance money from her father?" Percy asked.

"I think Leandros will be able to make sure the money goes to her. The fact is Joel Wakefield *was* killed. We have someone who confessed to the murder. Just because he was hired to kill him doesn't make him any less of a murderer. If the case goes to trial, he'll win. But I'm pretty sure the insurance company will settle, if they know Leandros is going to take them to court over this."

"What about the girl?" Cleveland asked. "Is she going to stay on at the commune?"

"And if she does," added Percy, "won't she give her money to that Twang person?"

I smiled at them both. "I dropped in on Twang before I came back to New York. That's why I took so long getting back here. I'm pretty sure he's not going to want her to stick around after what I told him about the murder case. I think he's going to ask her to leave."

Cleveland scratched his stubbly chin. He seemed relieved. "That's good."

I invited Detective Cleveland to join us for a glass of Prosecco but when he found out what it was, he declined, complaining about the paperwork he had to take care of.

I still wouldn't say he was smitten, but when we

shook hands I sensed in his gruff goodbye a surprising and pleasant respect for me.

49.

It turned out that Twang didn't have to send Ruby away; she left his commune of her own accord. I found this out because an administrator at Williams College called to verify my contact information. It seemed that Ruby had supplied my name as her emergency contact.

"Does that mean she's enrolled for her last semester?" I asked. "She'll graduate in the spring?"

"Yes, of course."

I pressed further. "She's there now?"

"The semester starts next week. Everything seems to be in order for her courses. Her tuition for her senior year was paid in full last summer and she's registered for classes."

I was overjoyed. We hung up and I asked Percy if he could find a cell number for Ruby. Within minutes he'd texted it to me. I called her right away.

"Ruby? It's Sati."

"Oh—hello."

"I just heard from your college that you're going back. I'm so glad."

"Yes, me too. I guess." She sounded far away.

"Where are you now, Ruby?"

"At my mom's. I'm flying east this weekend."

"Which airport?" I asked. "I'd like to meet you—I can drive you to your college."

"Wow." Her voice brightened. "Thanks. Albany's the closest. Do you really want to meet me there? I could get a bus."

"Yes, I want to meet you."

"That would be great."

"Text me your flight info, okay? I'll rent a car and head up there this weekend. I used to live in the Berkshires so it'll be fun for me."

When I hung up, I found Percy looking at me. "What?" I asked.

"You're going away?"

"Just for a weekend. I want to see Ruby again—let her know I care. I think it's important. She seems so fragile."

"But that means a bunch of cancellations again. Your clients are going to get upset."

"And there'll be less commission for you," I teased. "But I'll only go overnight."

"Okay." Percy sighed deeply, but he was looking a lot more cheerful. "Probably a good idea to see her. I'll take care of your schedule."

I wanted to take Ruby to Glass Mountain. It's one of my favorite places in the world, a place that fills me with mountain-strength and calm whenever I'm there. I wanted to share that serenity with Ruby. It's where I wanted to tell her the truth about her father: that he loved her with all his heart and wanted to be sure she was taken care of for the rest of her life.

And I hoped by the time I saw her, Leandros

would have good news about the insurance money too.

But mostly I just wanted to see her again and give her a hug.

50.

Even in January Glass Mountain looked fine. I parked by the side of the road, and Ruby and I set off along the muddy track. I had rarely encountered other hikers on this particular stretch, probably because it didn't go anywhere—just ended at a little plateau that overlooked the valley.

The unusual thaw had permeated all the way up here, and I was glad of my Wellingtons because the mud was thick and squishy. Dozens of chickadees darted in and out of the bare Russian olive and bittersweet. We filled our lungs with the breeze from the south which feels such a gift in winter.

I could tell Ruby felt the magic of the place too. She hummed lightly under her breath every now and then, as though she really enjoyed the hike.

"Ruby, did your mom tell you about your dad? That he wasn't murdered after all?"

She gave a quick nod, then said throatily, "I don't understand though. Why would he do something like that? Just because he didn't have any money?"

"He wanted to make sure you were taken care of

financially. He loved you very much."

"It seems an awful way to die," she muttered, trying not to cry.

"I know."

It had been a cold winter so far, but on this day there was a temporary respite and we were up to a balmy 40 degrees Fahrenheit. The sky was pallid and the wind, when it picked up, felt like cold stone. More snow was on the way, but right now as I looked down at the friendly valley all I saw was peace.

I took her hand in mine. "The main reason is that he wanted to leave you financially secure. You're going to inherit a million dollars."

"I don't want it."

Leandros had already successfully negotiated the life insurance, as I had hoped he would. It helped that John Henry was the broker, since it turned out that all he wanted was for Ruby to get the money too. He'd been afraid that if I discovered the truth—that Joel had killed himself—Ruby wouldn't receive it.

"You're going to get it anyway. And the first thing you're going to do is speak with a financial advisor."

To my surprise, she gave my hand a friendly squeeze, even though she still looked teary.

We had reached the small outcropping near the top of Glass Mountain. The valley spread like swathes of drapey pale fabric below us. Everything seemed to sparkle, the jiggling branches in the bright sunshine, glistening with melting snow. Two red-tailed hawks circled in the light breeze overhead.

"Ruby, we all go through difficult times. I've had a hard year myself."

"What happened?"

"A year ago a client asked me for help in trying to find her brother. He had wandered off—he had dementia—and no one knew where he was. I tried my best, but I couldn't locate him. We never did find him. I lost faith in my ability to be intuitive." I gulped some air, because it had been a long time since I'd spoken about this. "They never found him. I lost faith—I lost every idea that I could be intuitive. Being psychic was my livelihood, my only skill, it was who I was. And the gift left me completely. I didn't know what to do."

"What did you do?"

"I carried on as best I could. It still hasn't come back, but I'm trying to figure out other ways of consulting. I'm trying at least to get my confidence back."

"You're okay," she said, taking my hand. "And you *are* intuitive. I know you are."

"Maybe I just have to take it on faith now, instead of knowing."

"Well, *I* know."

We smiled at each other, and walked a little farther up the hill. "There's something about being here that always makes me feel peaceful," I said. "Even the breeze feels magical."

She closed her eyes, and her nose grew pink.

"It *is* nice," she agreed softly. "I wished you lived closer."

"When I lived in this area I always rented, but I used to think I'd like buy a small piece of land. Most of it's public in this valley, but there are bits here and there that are privately owned. I thought it would be fun to build a small cabin—a place to go where no one can find you."

"It sounds wonderful," she sighed. "But wouldn't you be lonely?"

I shook my head. "No... and anyway, I know it won't happen. I've got enough to manage with my house in New York. It's just a dream. But it's important to dream, Ruby. It's important to imagine things—to imagine better ways, finer places, greatness. To go beyond yourself and out of yourself. Imagination has the power to set you free from seemingly unbearable limitations. When you feel depressed, come here and imagine my little cabin with me, okay? And maybe one day you'll tell me about some of your own imaginings."

"I will."

"Money doesn't set you free. Nor does getting a degree, or running away... but your imagination does."

She broke into the first real smile I'd seen. It lit up her whole face. Her tone was teasing, light. "I *get* it, Sati. I really do."

51. Six weeks later, Percy and I had settled into a good routine. I saw three clients between nine and one each day. Then we had a light lunch together, and caught up on some accounts, promotional ideas, follow-up to emails.

My bank account grew fatter every day. By the middle of February, I didn't have to be anxious about paying bills anymore. And Percy's ability to spread the word about my consulting services was so effective that sometimes I was booked two or three weeks in advance.

I could hardly believe my good fortune, and dreaded the day that his cast was going to be removed and he'd return to his old job.

But when the cast came off, he said he didn't want to go back—he wanted to remain where he was, working for me.

Much as I wanted him to, I tried to talk him out of it.

"There's no future in it for you," I said. "You could be CEO of a corporation by the time you're thirty if you followed the right path. Working for me will never get you anywhere."

He grinned. "Satyana, Incorporated. We'll see."

My cell rang and I saw it was Ruby. I hadn't heard from her in a while so I was glad to answer.

"Hello, Ruby! How are things?"

"I have to see you," she said, her voice sounding urgent. "It's really, really important."

My heart sank but I kept my voice calm and reassuring. "I'm here for you, Ruby. You know that. Where are you?"

I held my breath, hoping she wasn't back at Twang's commune.

"Let's meet at that place you took me to—Glass Mountain. I have a car now and can drive there. Can you come this weekend? Saturday?"

It was Thursday. "Are you sure you'll be okay till then? I can come sooner if you'd like."

"No, Saturday's good. Noon?"

"Okay, see you then."

I was anxious all the next day, concerned that something happened to her.

"There was something in her voice that makes me so nervous," I said to Percy. "Something's definitely up. I'm worried about her."

"What do you mean, 'something' in her voice?" he asked.

"A sort of hidden energy—like she was hiding something. I'm worried."

"I'll drive you," he offered.

I wasn't sure that was a good idea. "She wants to meet at this place which is quite a hike from the road. Do you think it's a good idea for your leg?"

"It's the best idea. I need to get back in shape. Were you going to rent a car? I'll arrange it."

"And I was going to stay over Saturday night with a friend who lives near there," I said. "Otherwise it's a whole day of driving."

"That sounds fine. I have friends too, or I'll stay at a motel. We can plan on being back Sunday afternoon."

52.

Just seeing Glass Mountain in the distance, especially with Percy driving smoothly and effortlessly along the winding road, made my heart sing. It rose in curving granite like a tree-covered mosque, two smaller mounds on either side of the large dome-like center. It was still coated in sugar-cube whiteness. Even Percy, who tended toward understatement, remarked that it looked good.

He parked the car at the bottom of the trail and we got out and stretched. I was still worried about his recently healed fracture, but he assured me he was fine, and if it started to ache, he'd brought a brace. I knew his enforced immobility had bothered him enormously, but I hadn't realized how athletic he was until I saw him stretching and touching his toes and looking really glad not to be on crutches.

A blue Camry was parked by the side of the road, but no sign of Ruby.

"She must have gone on ahead," I said.

"Then let's go."

We set off along the track. That's when I noticed deep indents of tires ground into the dark mud.

"Look at that," I said. "Cars never come up here. It's not really a road."

"Not cars—those are truck tires. A car would get stuck in the mud."

I was disappointed at the thought that my favorite hiking trail was being driven on by trucks.

We continued on, and the mud grew worse. We couldn't even stay on the road, but made our way through the snowy grass by the side of what now seemed more of a road than a trail.

We wended through a thick grove of maples, but even here the road seemed to have widened … we wound around the side of the hill … and …

My jaw dropped.

There, exactly in the spot I had always imagined it, was the sweetest tiny house I had ever seen. A stone path led from the road to a bright orange front door. The walls were mostly of glass, and the trim as pink as strawberry ice cream. A tiny metal spiral staircase led up to the rooftop terrace.

I gave a little scream of excitement.

The freshly-painted door opened, and Ruby came out smiling, her red hair loose and gleaming in the sunshine.

"There you are! *Finally*!" She skipped over to me and gave me a huge bear hug.

Her hug took my breath away, which was already having a hard time getting into my lungs from the surprise.

"This is Percy," I introduced him. "He drove me."

They shook hands, but Ruby was much more

interested in my reaction to the house, and Percy wanted to look at it.

"Come on!" Ruby said, practically bouncing with excitement. "I want to show you the inside. But careful not to touch the walls—some of the paint is still wet."

It was much more than a cabin—this was a real miniature house. It consisted of a single room with large picture windows that overlooked a wide open porch and the valley beyond. It was snuggled against the back of the mountain to the north, keeping it protected from most storms. There was a small sleeping loft over the kitchen area. I poked my head up there and saw that it was spacious enough to sit up in and it even had a porthole window overlooking the front path.

"You did it!" I breathed. I had never seen anything more darling in my life. "You *imagined*."

"No, *you* imagined," she corrected me. She pressed something hard into my glove and I looked down. It was a shiny silver key. "It's for you."

I stared at the key in my hand, then lifted my eyes to meet hers as realization set in. *A gift.* "I can't take this. Sweetheart, you really need to manage your money—I—"

She laughed, closed my hand over the key.

"It's my senior project. You're going to have to let some people come and see it before they'll let me graduate, but I'll try to arrange that for when you're not here. And once I've graduated, no one has to come here ever again, except for you and whoever you invite. It's your own private little heaven, just like you said you always wanted."

"It's incredible," I gasped. "But how did you do it?"

"I found out who owned this bit property—it's not much, just an acre, but everything around is protected so you won't have neighbors. And I wanted to buy you furniture, but then I thought you'd probably have more fun doing that yourself. Anyway, less is more, right?"

"What about water?" Percy asked as we went back outside.

"We dug a well and it uses a hand-pump. Solar panels for light. I hope, anyway. And there's a composting toilet."

"Brilliant," he said, impressed. I could tell that from my description of Ruby he had not believed she'd be capable of a surprise like this.

"When I graduate I'm going to start a tiny house business," she told me. "What do you think?"

"Fabulous."

"Yes, I'm so excited."

"I can't believe it," I said. "It's all too much."

"Sati, you gave me much more than just a house." She put her arms around me and buried her face in my throat. Her throat caught. "You freed me … from myself."

Percy was climbing up the tiny spiral stairs to the stargazing roof.

"Come on up," he called.

I could tell he was as excited as Ruby.

We followed him up the metal stairs to the walled roof. It was empty except for two Adirondack chairs.

"You *did* get furniture!" I protested.

"Oh, these old things! While the construction guys were here I had them throw them up here. Otherwise I thought it might be hard to get them up the stairs. They're so heavy."

"It's a fantastic place," Percy said.

As we gazed around, the deep blue sky seemed to swell protectively and tenderly. I imagined being up here with a telescope on starry nights and laughed out loud.

"I still can't believe it."

"You had no idea I was going to do this?" Ruby asked. "I decided when we were here last time."

"No, I really had no idea."

"And you say you're psychic!" she teased.

Winslow Eliot is a writer and teacher who has published thirteen books of fiction, non-fiction, and poetry. Her work has been published in twenty countries and translated into eleven languages. Like her newest heroine, Winslow is a gifted intuitive who reads cards & palms, and loves a good mystery.

Find out more about her at winsloweliot.com.

Photo: Sarah Dinan

If you'd like to learn more about the marvelous world of intuitive consulting, especially the lenormand and tarot cards, there are many excellent resources, books, groups, teachers, communities, and helpers. Here are some places online to get you started:

Carrie Paris at carrieparis.com
Donnaleigh Rose at divinewhispers.net
Caitlin Matthews at hallowquest.org.uk
Madame Jozefa Seaqueen at seaqueen.wordpress.com
Melissa Hill at sassysibyl.com
Rana George at ranageorge.com
Ruth and Wald Amberstone at the tarotschool.com
Sheilaa Hite at sheilaahite.com
and many, many more ...

This list is just a place to begin – you'll find groups, courses, and communities just by opening this magical door a tiny bit...

And if you'd rather continue your exploration in the smartly-gloved hands of Satyana, she'll be back soon with her next adventure: **Sati and the Clover.**